Contents

1

CHARLENE BLUE

LOVE, THEE ELITE 2
BY CHARLENE BLUE

Must read

(Prologue)

Major returned home with only one person on his mind. However, explaining himself was far from simple. Females from Major's past kicked up chaos, losing every battle, some with their own lives.

Members of Thee Elite all came together in love and marriage. They are now proud parents of the next generation. However, being tiny kids. The sneaky old Great-greats thinks training the inner darkness should begin now!

Jamie and English both got rude awakenings. But did it stick, or are there more outsiders instigating more profound plans to take the families down once and for all? Will the learned lessons keep the nightmares away? Are all threats from the White family over? Or will hopes of entanglements break up happy homes?

Chapter 1: Jamie Winters (White)
Five years ago, two months after (Major & JLynn's wedding.)

"**W**ho are you, and how did you get into my room?" I asked the stranger standing at my bedside.

"Hello, Jamie, my name is Billion, and I'm your brother."

"What? Billard didn't have any sons. So who are you really?"

"I guess he wanted it to be kept a secret. And from what I can tell, it causes you much confusion."

"Yeah, well, confused is one thing shocked, not so much! Billard is full of cryptic secrets that explode like time bombs."

"Consider me one of those bombs! I'm here because a little birdie told me you have information that can make our family wealthy!" Billion boasted.

"Ha! You need to tell your little birdie to stop fuckin lyin!"

"I want you to tell me everything you know about the five families." He commanded.

"They're fucking dangerous, and you need to stop while you're ahead!" This dummy has been misinformed. There is no way in hell I'm opening up that pandora's box again.

"That's just it. I was sent special instructions from our father to look into those five families and destroy them! His journal states that they live on land that initially belongs to us!" Billion informed.

"How so?" I asked,

"That's what I'm trying to figure out! Billiard said there is an original will naming his older brother, the beneficiary."

"Now that sounds fishy because his brother was a twin also. Why wouldn't both the twins' names be on this so-called will? Look, it seems to me you don't have any proof whatsoever. You give me the impression of being an intelligent guy. Why don't you cut your losses and move on with your life? I askekd.

"It's not just the wealth I'm concerned with. I feel those people are responsible for our family's demise. Aren't you the least bit curious about that?" He questioned with an accusatory stance. Not really, I say under my breath.

"If you think for one minute, I'm going to let these nig…."

"Don't say it, mutha fucker!"

"Like I was saying, I'm not going to stand by and watch them live happily ever after on what rightfully belongs to me!" Billion spat.

"Ahh! I see! It's all about you! Now we're getting somewhere. Have you spoken to anyone else besides your birdie and me?"

"Are you going to help or not?" Billion ignored my question. *"I'm aware of our father's sick and twisted genes. And judging by your patched-up wounds. His sins are the reason you're in here, all fucked up! Don't let it be in vain, Jamie!"* He snidely retorted.

All the bullshit I put my family through is ridiculous. Since they didn't throw me to the wolves and write me off as collateral damage. I am forever indebted to them. I was recently released from the ICU unit after being stabbed 32 times. I'd say I was truly blessed with a second chance. As long as I stay on my meds. If not, there is no point in returning for me.

However, I'm going to pretend to work with Billion and report all my findings to my mother. I'm sure that will earn extra brownie points with them. Maybe just maybe, Major will give me a pat on the back or somewhere else! Fuck let me take my meds!

Chapter 2: Major Forest

"Ooooooh! Majorrrrrrrrrr! Please go faster! I'm dying over here. Stop torturing me! Baby, please!!!!! Ahh ah ah noooooo! Why did you slow down again?" ILynn whimpered,

"Put your hands back on the bedpost, ILynn." I moved in and out of ILynn as slow as possible! Why am I doing this? Let me tell you! Miss ILynn is not at all innocent in this game of fuckery. At four in half years old, our daughter MayLynn wakes up at 7am every morning like clockwork.

So, my petty ass wife thinks it's funny to hop on my member 15 minutes before seven, knowing damn well I last longer than that. As soon as MayLynn's little feet hit the floor, running towards our room. ILynn hops off my shit and laughs. Like having blue balls isn't a real thing! So right now, I'm getting her back for the blue balls I've sported all week!

"I'm so sorry, baby, I won't ever do that again. Now, please!" She screamed loudly. I sped up, and her muscles clenched, telling me she was ready! Picking up the pace. I accepted ILynn's apology causing her to violently erupt like a volcano! "Damn! I bet you won't fuck with me again, uh? I taunted. ILynn just turned to the side and let sleep claim her.

While ILynn slept, I went downstairs and made dinner. I prepared MayLynn's favorite dish. Orange chicken, rice, broccoli, and eggrolls.

"Yay! Daddy, thank you so much! Kelly is going to be furious; she didn't get any of this delicious food. This is her favorite meal also!" MayLynn fussed.

"Don't worry about it. We'll invite Kelly over the next time a make it, okay?"

"Okay, Daddy, now let's say grace and eat before mommy wakes up! She says the long prayer, and my stomach growls the whole time!" MayLynn says without cracking a smile.

"Uhh! How yall just gonna eat without me!"

"Hi! Mommy! We already said grace! Right, daddy? MayLynn's eyes landed on me, looking like (the bulging eye) emoji.

I laughed at ILynn's hurt expression because she knows how long-winded she is. I'm in awe of ILynn and my daughter and couldn't be more proud. They are my survival kit!

"Baby, your phone is going to vibrate off of the counter."

Hopping up to retrieve my phone. I can see a slight attitude on ILynn's face. The family has been working with a new Ally that just so happens to be another female.

The only difference is I never had a relationship with Tyra, and most importantly, we never slept together. I would never throw away my family for a simple piece of ass! I just wish my wife knew that.

"ILynn, say what you need to say. I don't do the whole side-eye, shit." "I just don't like the way she looks at me when I come around." She shrugged. "And how's that," I asked. "It's like she wants me to think yall did something other than the mission. Like she's keeping a big secret."

"Come here, ILynn!" I guided her to sit on my lap. Your intuition may be right about her actions. But your only concern should be my reaction. I can assure you nothing has ever happened and never will! I love you!

We just need to make like a knot that nobody can untie or loosen." (Charlene Blue made me say this corny shit!) Finally, answering my phone. My pops voice boomed through the phone, confirming the obvious.

"I need you to go to Germany and do a sweep of Martha's safe house. A white wolf was kicking up dirt and recruited a pack! Your Aunt B is already posted up in the house next door, waiting on your arrival."

I can hear ILynn in the background, laughing! She met my Auntie B last year! Needless to say, My aunt, Bobbye, is fucking insane! You thought Kiley was off her rocker! Shiiiiiiiiiiiiiiiiiiit! (Isiah Whitlock Jr.). Kiley is a heads type of gal, and Auntie B, wellllllllllllll!

"Tyra will be there with the weapons. Capture, question, and kill!" Rumond finalized.

"Baby, can you get my bags ready? I have to leave in a few hours. I should only be there for a couple of days! I'll give you all the details once I have them."

As ILynn, descended down the stairs with my bags. I decided to take a family boat ride across the lake.

"Are those new people moving into the Gruffs house? ILynn asked. "Yeah, Jaylin and I have a bet going to see how long it takes before another for sale sign goes up." I laughed.

The Gruffs brutally murdered each other in that house a few years ago! It's believed to be haunted, but some people think it's bullshit. Hell! Something is going on in that house if nobody can occupy it no longer than three months.

"Hey, there goes 3G Victorious walking into the garden

nursery. HI! 3G!" MayLynn yelled and waved.

"What is that old man up to now?" I asked ILynn. "Shit, who knows! I saw him leaving Miss Janine's house the other morning! Like does it even still work at 96 years old?" We both laughed!

"How deep is the lake, mom?" MayLynn asked. "It's deep, so you don't need to go near it without supervision. Do you hear me?"

"Yes, Ma'am! Daddy! Who is that man taking pictures of us?" MayLynn scarcely asked. I looked down at MayLynn, and her eyes were as black as mine!

Chapter 3: Landin Forest

As soon as all of our children started walking. I went out and bought a church van! ILynn's cousins hooked it up with chrome everything! So I've made it my civic duty to take all the Black – Eye – Pea kids to Sunday school every Sunday! No! I am not kidding. Everybody thinks this shit is a gift, and I do not! I'm not quite sure how to get used to it because my little Kelly has it. So, if the darkness resides in them. JESUS is going to be sitting right next to it!

My first stop is Jaylin's house. Bella's been on some sneaky shit lately, and she better hope for her sake Jaylin never finds out about it.

"Hey! Uncle Landin!" Jr. yelled, making me jump a little! Damn, he's loud!

"You ready little dude?"

"Yep! Bye, Mom and Dad!"

"Yall good?" I asked. "Yeah, man, I need to holla at you

when you drop him back off." Jaylin insisted.

"Alright."

Next stop Kiley and Ashton. I honked because both Kelly and Jr. are in their own little worlds.

"What up dough Uncle Landin?" Kyle said to me.

"What up, slick! Where's your sister?"

"She is in there trying to sneak her Adidas out the window!" I bent over, laughing hard as hell because just then, a pair of sneakers flew out of Ashley's window!

Damn, if she isn't a replica of Kiley! "Let's go, Ashley, before ya momma whoops you!" Looking at the shiny white shoes she's wearing, I would sneak some different shoes, too. "Ut! Oh! Here she comes!" I warned! "Ashley, what do you have in your hands!" "DRIVE UNCLE, DRIVE!" Ashley yelled, and I did just that!

Next, stop Major and ILynn's. "Oh, look, little Chris is over here!" Kelly chirped. Chris is Angel and Christian's three-year-old son! When I tell you he loves going to church, I mean it! He probably knows the Bible better than me! MayLynn grabbed Chris's hand and walked to the van!

"Good Morning! Kiddos!"

"Good Morning! Blessed be the day!" Chris said. See what I mean, what three years old, you know, says things like that!

"Why couldn't we just come with Nanna Rose and Grandmother Elanor for regular service? Our Sunday school teacher's breath smells like coffee and cigarettes!" My daughter Kelly fussed!

"Look, yall need all the church yall can get trust me!" "UH! Uncle Landin, why are there two cars following us? One is supposed to be there, but the other one is not!" Jr. assessed.

I immediately called security so they could inform Jaylin of us being followed. I looked in the rearview mirror and pushed the pedal to the metal! The black button-eye kids were in full defense mode and in desperate need of some Blessed oil!

Chapter 4: Jaylin Forest

Five years ago, I thought I married the woman I wanted to spend the rest of my life with. Today I'm trying my best not to strangle her and make her wildflower fertilizer. Our son barely sees his mother because she uses my work as an excuse to step out! What do I mean by stepping out? I'll let her tell you.

"How long are you going to give me the silent treatment Jaylin?" I sighed because she was getting on my fucking nerves.

"Let's not pretend there isn't a reason for me ignoring your lying ass!"

"Well, this is just ridiculous, Jaylin; you need to stop this. I don't understand why you have a problem with me working!" She pressed, throwing her nose up in the air which made me laugh at her sarcastic comment.

"I never had or have a problem with you working. It's precisely what we were doing when we met back up! But what you are not going to do is make this about me."

"Jalin, you work so much you barely make love to me or kiss me, for that matter. And here lately, you look at me as if I smell like a skunk! So I took on extra shifts to feel needed."

I started laughing my ass off! "I give you everything you need and want, Bella! I am on vacation now for three weeks. Because you asked me for more time." She tried to interrupt, but I deaded that shit. "When I told you the next day, I'm all yours. What did you say? You were just kidding. Like my job isn't paramount to the air, we fucking breathe."

"That's not fair, Jay!" She snarls.

"What's not fair? Me taking off to spend time with my wife, or me not lining up with the bullshit you got going on? You haven't made it home on time to read Jr.'s bedtime stories in months. I mean, you talk about how you barely see me. While your son is saying the same thing about you!" Bella's phone was buzzing in her pocket, so what I just said went in one ear and out the other.

"Well, what do you want from me? I'm already late for my 10 o clock appointment for Renea."

"You do know this is Sunday, right? Since when is your dentistry open on Sundays?" I quizzed.

"As of today, I started accepting appointments only!" She

shrugged.

"Yeah! Alright." Done with this conversation.

"What? What do you want me to do, Jaylin?" "I want you to get your lying ass out of my face."

"Stop being such a dick, Jay. I can't and won't take it anymore." Well, stop pretending like you can!" She didn't like my undercurrent, but I didn't give a fuck. Bella's shit is catching up to her, and she will not like the outcome of my rage! My phone beeped, but before I answered it, I left Bella with these words.

"Let me find out you have a death wish!"

"Whatever, Kendra is there waiting on me!"

I didn't even correct her because clearly, Bella forgot she told me Renea had an appointment, not Kendra. See, it's gotten to the point where she fails to keep up with her own lies.

After Bella left, I went back into my man cave to queue up video footage! Landin called earlier, concerned about another car following them. I eased his mind by telling him of my decision to amp up security. A storm is coming, and we need to be prepared. I heard my door chirp, so I just called for him to meet down here. Jr. wanted to go with his Nanna Rose, so I'll have plenty of time to discuss things with my brother.

"You might need to go grab some tums or 7-up before I

push this button," I said warning Landin.

"Nigga hit the button! I'm good!" Bluuuuuha! Who the fuck called Auntie B? How does she wipe her ass with those long-ass fingernails?" Landin asked.

"I'm going to rewind this Shit to the beginning."

-----------In Germany---------

Aunti B: "Ugh! My nephew is taking too long! They really didn't need to have him come all the way out here. I'm just going to go over there!" Knock! Knock!

"Who are….." RAT TAT TAT TAT TAT TAT TAT TAT TAT TAT TAT TAT TAT TAT TAT TAT TAT TAT TAT TAT PEW PEW PEW TAT TAT TAT TAT! Ooh, blue ones. Oh! My! Green ones are my favorite! Pluck pluck! Ugh! Those are contacts! Pluck pluck pluck pluck…………………

Chapter 5: Major Forest

My flight was delayed for 45 minutes. Knowing this was a time-sensitive mission. I had my cousins hack a few traffic lights! Tyra and I arrived at the same time. Which was great because that meant I didn't have to meet her at the hotel. With the news, ILynn brought to my attention. I mustn't confuse things going forward! Getting out of the car simultaneously, Tyra pushed her breast up with a sly grin. She proceeds to flirt with her body walking slow to her trunk, making sure I get a full view of her apple-shaped ass.

"You ready handsome?" I didn't speak. I just grabbed what I needed and walked to the door.

"Auntie B, you in here?" I asked, but there was no reply!

"Surely she wouldn't leave the post, I mean...."

"Shh!" I quieted Tyra's annoying statement. Stalking off into the guest room facing the house next door. My antennas went up! Once I had my silencers secured, I walked up to the back door. The stillness gave me goosebumps as I neared.

If I was a scary nigga, I would have jumped at my Auntie B's voice. This woman was sitting on one of the high ceiling beams like an Eagle watching her prey. I then took the time to check out the scene, and that's when I noticed a pile of at least twelve guys over in the corner!

"Wow! Are those…"

" EYEBALLS!!!" Tyra took my words from me. Over on the counter sits a baby blue mini-sized Yeti cooler. The contents inside were full of my Aunties' most prized possessions on ice.

"Hey! Take her weak stomach having ass out of here! She's about to vomit on my collections." I didn't have to turn around to see Tyra running out of the house.

"I mean, she's the weapon supplier, right? Why not supply them and take yo ass home? Why stick around? She's obviously not built for this shit! Let me find out she got the hots for you, Nephew!" I just shook my head.

"Antie B, did you question any of the guys before you killed them?" My aunt is a certified #bonkthefuckout! #shecrazyasfuck! #dontsaythewrongthingorelse! Type of person. Great Grand Raymond decided to go ahead and train her alongside my Grandfather, Red. He was 19 when the Elite was established. Auntie B was 16 and was a busy bee, very much like Kiley!

After Auntie B completed training, There started to be complaints of a Negro girl snatching out white men's eyes and running off with a sinister laugh! When descriptions of her began to circulate. Raymond had to send her away to California to live with his mother's family. Did things get better? FUCK NO! She became a serial eye plucker!

"I left you one guy in the room! He should be able to tell us something!" She said nonchalantly. I took the picture out of my pocket, ready to get some answers on who hired him. Walking into the room, her long sharp stiletto nails directed me to. A man with a black sack on his head, was moaning out in pain. When I pulled it off, I put my head down. This dude's eyeballs are out there in that cooler! He won't be able to identify shit!

"Auntie B! How exactly is he going to see this photo?" I held the picture in my hand, waiting on a rocket scientist's answer.

"Well, what's the guy's name? maybe he can tell you that way, genius!" she pressed.

"Do you honestly think he used his real name?" I asked.

"Damn, you gotta point. Well, get his phone; maybe he has information in there."

We grabbed his phone, and the muthafucker had a retina scan on it!

"Fuck! Do you remember which eyes belong to him? Because if not, we're going to be scanning eyeballs all night!" I fussed.

"Calm down, little lad! He had green eyes! And you know those are my favorite, so they shouldn't be hard to find! Only three of them had green eyes. Ah, here you go; these should be it!"

I looked at my Auntie like she'd lost the other half of her mind. I just held the phone up, hoping she'd get the point of me not wanting to touch them.

"Jeez! Loosen up; they're just eyes, Major. You act like they're going to see you to death!" She hilariously laughed at her own joke. Beep! The phone opened.

"See there, that wasn't so hard, was it?"

I don't know if we're lucky or blessed to always reveal a wolf in sheep's clothing, but I'll take Blessed for 300 Alex! Mr. no eyes possessed pictures and videos dating back five years. Someone is definitely talking because there are pictures of us down to our kids! And that's where I draw the line! Showing Auntie B his phone, she began to pace the floor!

"Wake-up! Muthafucker!" No eyes jolted out in pain! "Who sent you, and don't lie because I will pluck your tongue out next!"

"Okay! Okay, two women approached me five years ago, wanting to know If I would look into you all! However, one of the women was more forthcoming with vital information. She sounded like a scorned woman!

I refused at first until they threatened to harm my sister! She is a beautiful young Afro-German woman any man would kill for. When I reached out to warn her, it was too late! The couple threatened to pimp her out in the United States until I completed surveillance. However, my plans changed once I located my sister turning tricks in a ritzy strip club. With intentions of running, I found a replacement, but he disappeared!"

I smiled because I definitely took care of that peeping tom after our family boat ride.

"So, why are you here?" I asked.

"I got a phone call instructing me to drop off all of my findings to this location. When I arrived, all of these men were present, awaiting instructions. I was just about to leave when the gunfire started. I hid in the closet, but I tried to make a run for it!" He howled out in pain!

Auntie B grabbed a syringe of morphine from her bag and jabbed it into his neck! When the pain began to subside, he went on to explain.

"Did you ever retrieve your sister?" I asked.

"No! I almost didn't recognize her at first. She must've bleached her skin! She told me she was happy and to go on with my life."

"Damn!" Before the morphine took effect, he revealed the women hiring a man named BJ Barny Jingle Whipsickles, or something like that. When my eyes met Auntie B's, we fell out laughing!!!! Why are we laughing? You'll find out!

Chapter 6: Bella Banks-Forest

"Yes! Right there, baby, Ooooooh! Shit, you thick bitches know how to ride! My lover boasted. I love fucking him because I feel in control! And plus, I love the attention! As a matter of fact, I thrive on it! If it's not about me, and only me, I get creative! BJ is so easy, and he fits my sweet peach! I don't need to be pushed past my limits! Or stretched out beyond repair. No, this right here is simple, fun, and entertaining!

Right now, I'm straddling BJ on the dentist's chair, and his hands are gripping my hips and moving me in a circle! My lips quivered as I exploded for the third time!

"Ah!!!!!" And so does he! BJ came in for teeth cleaning several years ago! It was something about him that made me instantly hot! Maybe it was how he stared me down the whole time he was here. His visits were so frequent he finally beat the bush and asked me out.

Ignoring my wedding ring and the shameful glares of my employees, he made it his mission to make my fantasies come true! I know you're thinking I'm stupid for jeopardizing my marriage with my handsome, powerful husband! But he doesn't pay enough attention to me! Work....Work....Work. That's all he does. He thinks I didn't catch on to that nagging statement of me not handling his dick!

My comfort zone was pushed beyond belief when we first had sex! I mean, my pussy was in shock! I didn't complain and took it like a champ only because the attention and affection were out of this world. It was like he craved me every minute of the day! All that came to an end when our son Jaylin Jr. was born. Don't get me wrong, I love my son. It's just that I love being the center of it all more!

You would think I was well adjusted to my husband by now. JR was 9lbs, and I still couldn't fit Jaylin's mandingo inside of me! I knew he'd be frustrated at times. However, I could barely walk after sex, and that's why he asked if I wanted to get surgery to open me up a little more. But I refused defeat. BJ's tool is a thick 71/2, and that is perfect for me! Turn your lip up at me all you want. It's my kitty!

There is no way Jaylin knows what I'm up to because his job comes first. I often wonder where all that work was when my parents were killed. They call my husband the watcher. But who watched over them when they were gunned down in

London!

After they died, I shut the whole family out! Even my cousins Ashton and Christian. They didn't really deal with me anyway because of my bratty ways.

Our grandparents passed away a year after each other of natural causes. Being the oldest and only girl, I felt I should've received a higher inheritance amount! Instead, $600 Million was split evenly between me, Ashton, and Christian. The hell I raised had them looking at me differently ever since. But I didn't care.

"Hey, where did your mind go, baby? Come back and sit on my face!"

BJ loves to lick my honey pot, so I just closed my eyes and imagined it being my husband's long thick tongue! It's smooth yet aggressive! It's commanding, eager, and thirsty! One flicker from Jaylin would take you out!

My moans were so loud my ears started to ring causing me to open my eyes. I stopped mid-swirl. I started to have a mini panic attack because there was a shadow of a tall figure standing in the hallway of my dentistry. I hopped off of Bj's face to get a closer look, but nothing was there!

I ran to the front doors to see if I may have forgotten to lock them.

"What the hell is going on, Bella?" BJ questioned. "I'm just double-checking the locks! I thought I saw someone standing in the hallway!" BJ began to laugh while I was freaking the hell out!

"That's your conscious fucking with you, Bella!" Bj taunted.

Out of my peripheral, there was the most beautiful bouquet of colorful wildflowers I've ever seen!

"Oh! My! Gosh! BJ! Why didn't you tell me you got me flowers! These are amazing!" I turned to give him a kiss, but he just stared at me with his right eyebrow arched!

"I didn't buy those, Bella." He revealed, gathering his clothes. "And they weren't sitting on that counter when I walked in here either!"

"Stop playing BJ. It's not funny!" I giggled.

"I'm not, and I'm dead serious." He assured, now fully dressed.

"Then who...........?"

Chapter 7: JLynn Cross-Forest

I'm sitting here impatiently waiting for my husband's return, and MayLynn is driving me mad about her food containing too much seasoning! Now don't get it twisted; I also can throw down in the kitchen. But apparently for this four-year-old. (I don't have the sauce.)

"Did you read the directions first? It's too tangy, mommy! You put too much orange marmalade in it! Daddy said, you only need a little bit for orange chicken." She complained.

I wish I would've said some shit like this to my mom! She would've slapped me back into my dad's sperm count!

"Well! MayLynn, you have one option. Wash it off and eat it because I am not going to make you anything else!"

"Fine, I'm just going to eat the noodles then." She shrugged.

"No, you're going to eat everything on your plate, May-Lynn!"

"But...." "Do what your Mom says, May," Major says from

the front door!

Man, my husband is fine as hell! And how he slipped in here all heroic will get him a back rub and a lot of DT time!

"Okay! Dad!" MayLynn rolled her eyes. But I saw it! I noticed a strained look on Major's face, and I didn't like it! I also don't want to assume anything, so I asked, seemingly concerned.

"We have to amp up security again. We've been under surveillance for five years."

"By who?" I asked.

"By someone who feels this land rightfully belongs to them. I believe we know who it is, but due to adverse circumstances, namely my crazy ass, Auntie! We weren't able to get visual confirmation!"

"Wow! What did she do? Or do I want to know?" I laughed. Major's Auntie B is a maniac!

I never once thought I'd meet someone like Kiley, but the universe has a way of shocking the shit out of people! It was Great Grand Raymond's 93rd Birthday when this pecan brown woman with lustrous white hair came strolling throw the dining room! Her almond-shaped ice gray eyes looked like mystical rain clouds! (It makes sense to me, so roll with it!) Her lips were plump with matte ruby red lipstick and dimples in both cheeks. She was stunning!

I swear having dinner with this group never goes without surprises. I don't know if they were expecting Auntie B to make an appearance. But when I looked at a concerned Major holding a pair of sunglasses, I got nervous. *"Put these on, baby. I'll explain later!"* Only he didn't have to explain because the reasoning behind it all unfolded right in front of me!

"Oh! My! Gosh! Green ones are my favorite!" She boasted while holding Sage's face delicately in her extraordinarily long stiletto nailed hands! What I saw next had me wailing in laughter over the arm of my chair! Landin must of ran track, jumped hurdles, and did the long jump in school! Because the way he made it to the table was absolute magic!

"So! Nobody was going to save my wife's eyes from being plucked out of her sockets!" Landin angrily spat!

"Oh! Boy, shut up, I was just looking! You're jumping over furniture like a black cat with its tail on fire!" Auntie B heckled.

"You would have flipped out to if a black white-haired-looking wizard was looking into your husband's face like that! It looked like you were going to suck out her soul!"

We all laughed uncontrollably. When Auntie B looked up and realized Angel, and I had on sunglasses, she bent over in a fit of giggles!

"Damn! ILynn? Did you use the whole jar of marmalade?" Major asked, jolting me out of memory lane!

"See! Mommy, I told...."

I gave her a look my mom gave me at her age, and she shut right the hell up! Right or wrong, I don't play that shit! I gave Major a look also. Don't be calling me out in front of her! O'l black olive eye twins! After three texts, messages appeared on my cell. Angel starts calling!

Chapter 8: Angel Mirez-Banks

"**G**IRLLLLLLL! You are not going to believe how much money CJ has in his (Bad Word Jar)!"

"How much?" ILynn laughs!

"$700 fuck...."

"Uh! Mom!" CJ says with his hand out!

"$701! Do I cuss that much!" "YES!" both ILynn and CJ say at the same time! I got up and walked to the back of my house. "I mean, he's three; how the hell does he know what curse words are anyway?!" "Did you really just ask me that?" ILynn responded.

"You know what? The next time MayLynn is over here. I'm going to bring up the idea of making you a fucking swear jar! You are the sailor of all sailing curse words! How about that? You'll hit a $1,500 before this Friday!" I say in triumph!

"No! You know who would be a rich kid?" ILynn asked. "KELLY!" We both said at the same time!

"Bitch she would be a millionaire with Landin's mouth!

I talked to Ilynn a few more minutes after she told me what MayLynn said about her cooking! Our kids are from another dimension! My son is three and can quote the Bible like nobody's business! And obviously, he's a money collector as well! I'd just finished putting the one-dollar bills back in the jar when I got a text message from an unknown. It read: When the hats lurk, the Kitties twerk! 69.

I didn't know what that fuck that meant, so I just wrote it off as someone having the wrong number.

"Hey, babe, how was your day!" I asked Christian. Lately, I've been thinking back on how I almost lost him for good! Once it all settled in and I saw the era of my ways. He'd started dating someone else! When I tell you, she wasn't a scrub. Believe me! She was a chocolate beauty, but the exposed accent she tried to hide was evident.

I remember vividly. I was moping around in the salon when I took a phone call from Victorious! He said,

"You better put a smile on that face before I come in there and do it for you! All you need is a veil and a box of tissues, and I'd

think you were at a funeral!"

I looked up, and for sure! Victorious was sitting in front of the salon with a binocular over his one eye! "Victorious! Does grandpa Victor Sr. know you're driving his Maybach?

"No, and you're not going to tell him, are you?"

"No, of course not!" I lied because I was going to call him as soon as I got off this phone!

"I need a lineup, and I need you to shave this beard off."

"Why didn't you just come in here?" I asked.

"I wasn't sure if you were here, and I didn't want to have to walk all the way back to the car! He said, mosying in the salon!

It just amazes me how youthful Victorious and Raymond remain to be. At 96 years old, they both still have a head full of hair and full beards! Whatever youth juice they're drinking, I want it!

"Look at you all skinny and shit from not eating and crying over that nigga! You better get it together because this person standing here is not my Great Grandchild!"

Victorious is right; I need to stop moping. I lined Victorious up, trimmed his nose hairs, and shaved his beard! He now looks like a young Billy D Williams!

"Thanks! Baby girl! Now listen, I was at the bank before I came

here, and I overheard Christian making plans with a young lady!
The girl had on a catsuit with the biggest plump round a--"

"Victorious!" I shouted, not wanting to hear the description.

"Well, anywho, he made plans to take her to Lemons chicken.
With that being revealed, do you want him or not, and if you do?
You need to get your head out of your ass and get creative!"

I did just that. I took my ass down to that restaurant with
rollers in my hair and a nightgown stuffed with pillows and an attitude the size of Texas! As soon as I spotted them in the corner of
the restaurant, I got to work!

"CHRISTIAN! CHRISTIAN, I KNOW YOU ARE NOT ON A DATE
WHEN I'M PREGNANT WITH YOUR CHILD!"

Victorious was right. This bitch had a triple-stacked ass and
no waist! Hell naw!

"Wer ist des hundin!" (Who is this bitch!) The ho snapped
under her breath!

"Beobachten sie Ihren Mund! (Watch your mouth!) nie anneh
men (Never assume!) Christin retorted.

You would've thought she swallowed her gum at what Christian responded to her in her language. She obviously didn't know
he knew how to speak the German language!

Christian's date gathered her cell and purse and got the hell out of dodge! I couldn't do anything but laugh. I mean, her ass had to catch up with the rest of her body as it jiggled out of the door. That's how huge it was!

I turned around to Christian glaring intently in my eyes. I didn't know whether to run or run!

"Sit down, baby!" I sat down, and Christian laughed so hard tears ran out of his eyes! I picked up ol' girls lemon pepper wigs and went to town! And that's how I got my man back!

"Are you ready to eat, baby? I made empanadas!" I told Christian.

"No! I just wanna sit here for a minute." Christian put his hands on his head, which is a clear sign of frustration!

"What's wrong, babe? You're scaring me!"

"I think our branch manager stole money from the bank, but I can't prove it!"

"WHAT? What do you mean? How does that even happen? How much was taken?" I asked.

"$200 Million and that's not even the kicker! The transaction itself is fucked up because they made it look like we gave it to them!" Christian huffed!

"What do you mean?"

"The withdrawals came from both my account as well as Ashton's! $100 Million apiece!"

"Come again!"

Chapter 9: Christian Banks

"Do you remember last year when Ashton and I were at odds about the new hire?" Christian asked.

"Yes, Yall didn't speak for weeks," Angel recalled.

"Well, the new hire was Bella's best friend! Terry was what you call a mean girl! We used to fool around, but she was an attention whore like Bella! So, I ended things.

Growing up, we never really fooled with Bella. She would have these fits if she wasn't getting the attention she needed. One time she made up this story about being abused. She watched an episode on Good Times when Penny was burned with an iron.

This idiot did it and ran to school, showing everyone! She must've forgotten my mother's sister was the 9th and 10th-grade counselor. Aunt Melissa called her out on her shit because she could tell the wounds were self-inflicted.

You know, when you touch a hot handle on the stove, it

makes you jump! Well, it seems as though she tapped her arm with the iron, but not enough to singe her skin. If you're being abused, your abuser is going to burn the fuck out of your skin!

Bella was pissed until she saw the look on her mother's face! It broke her to know her daughter would go that far for attention!"

"Wow! I had no idea she was like that!" Angel admitted.

"Was? Haven't you ever noticed how distant she is at our family functions? She doesn't sit with us or speak to us! Bella doesn't do well around beautiful women! That's why she keeps Jaylin away, so he won't be able to engage in conversation with you all!"

"Why would she be intimidated by us? She is stunning in her own right! I mean, has she ever looked in the mirror?" Angel asked.

"It's not that she doesn't think she's beautiful. Bella wants to be the one and only focal point of the room!"

"I wonder if Jaylin's ever called her out on it?" Angel quizzed.

"I think he's starting to realize something's off with her. He doesn't have that same gaze in his eyes when he looks at her! I was going to ask him about it but changed my mind. He holds things in until we're standing in front of the wood chipper!" I laughed.

"So, are you okay with your cousin being wildflower food?" Angel chirped.

"Angel, if I find out that bitch and her friend stole money from the bank. They are going to meet Samurai Sam over there behind the wall!"

"What up, Major! Did you find anything?" I asked anxiously through the phone.

"I found yall money in an offshore account in Switzerland. When I hacked into the camera of the bank. It mysteriously stopped recording on that day! However, there is a camera on the roof of the hat boutique across the street! So, I'll let you know what I come up with!

Chapter 10: Jamie Winters-White

I stayed true to my word all of two weeks! The news of Major and ILynn getting married on the lake made me go into a deep depression! I know I said I was done trying him, but the hope was still there! I thought if I fed him information on what my brother was doing, he would at least acknowledge my existence! Wishful thinking, I know!

What pissed me off and made me join my brother was when I ran into a snack display staring at Major at the grocery store.

I couldn't take my eyes off him. And even though I'd made a giant mess and needed help picking all the shit up! Majowalked right past me as if I didn't exist! I even called out to him, and his smooth operating ass kept on walking!

"Here, let me help you with that." A familiar voice sang to me. Oh! My! God! It was Sonny, my music teacher. The one to who I gave my virginity! Oh! How scrumptious! He resembles a thugged out Lance Cross!

"Well, hello there, it's been a long time. You look great!" I flirted.

"Yeah, and I see you're grown now!" He said as he looked me up and down while biting his bottom lip!

("Oh, he wants to eat you inside out," My pussy responded.)

"Well, thank you for helping me. You seem to be the only gentleman in this section"

"Yeah, no problem. You must've caused problems with ol dude because he looked right through you!"

"You saw that, uh? Let's not talk about him. What brings you to town? Last I'd heard, you moved to Dallas." I recalled, hoping he'd follow the direction of my conversation.

"I did. I had to get away from your crazy ass!" He laughed.

"Well, you never turned me down un...."

"Until you crossed the line!" Sonny cut me off.

"Did I? because you obliged all over that room!"

I'd broken into Sonny and his fiancé's house one night! I overheard Sonny arguing with her about her drinking. So, I figured she had a drinking problem. I knew Sonny's schedule down to a T.

After school was over, Sonny would go to the gym around the corner from his house. He would work out for about an hour in a

44

half and sit in the steam room for 20 minutes. One night I thought I'd try my luck at being adventurous. While sonny was at the gym, I slipped into his house.

Just as I thought, his fiancé Tammy had drunk half a bottle of wine! Adding insult to injury, I put a crushed sleeping pill in her wine glass. She made this shit so easy! I hid in the pantry and watched her turn the wine glass up, emptying the contents in her belly!

She didn't even try to get up! She just laid her head down on the table! At least she cooked the nigga a meal before she started drinking. I bolted out of the closet and lifted her head to see if she was indeed out! I ran and put his food in the microwave and had it out on the table. Just like clockwork, I heard the keys jingling in the doorknob!

When he spotted Tammy in her stooper, he shook his head and carried her off to bed. He then walked back into the kitchen, washed his hands, and ate! Once he finished, he jumped in the shower. Which gave me time to switch closets. I was now in his bedroom closet, waiting for him to come out. Ahhhh! I became drenched at the sight of his 9 1/2 inches.

Sonny grabbed a bottle of lotion sitting on his nightstand. Once, he got a good rhythm stroking his shaft. I eased out of the closet and put my warm wet mouth on his thick meat! His eyes popped open, and I immediately grabbed his sausage in between my teeth, warning him not to hit me or cause a scene!

"What the fuck are you doing here, Jamie!" Sonny whispered. I just continued to bring him into my throat!

Sonny's eyes rolled to the back of his head, and that's when he turned into an animal. He hiked me up on the dresser and pounded my insides like he was trying to knock a dent out of his car door! He then laid on the bed and made me ride his face, all while his fiancé slept inches away from us! Just the risk of her waking up made me wetter!

"Hey! Baby, I walked all over the store and couldn't find you. Who's this?"

"This is one of my old students. Jamie, meet my wife, Tammy."

Chapter 11: Jamie Winters-White

DING! DING! DING! "I'm coming!" Jeez, I can't even use the bathroom in peace. Wow! His ears must've been ringing! I just literally thought him up! Sonny moved back home a couple years ago with his wife, Tammy. To be honest, I'm surprised he married her with her being a drunk and all. I take that back. Tammy is a cash cow!

Her dad owns a Billion-dollar media company! Tammy's got it made sipping wine and collecting a hundred-thousand-dollar weekly allowance! I would marry her wino ass too!

"You didn't show up last night!" Sonny growled. "Show up to what, Sonny?" I asked, concerned. I had no idea what the fuck he was talking about!

"I sent you an invitation. You didn't get it?" He worriedly asked.

"Oh! That was from you? I'm sorry, I thought it was a ploy! I did something a few years ago that landed me in the hospital for quite some time. So, forgive me if I'm a little paranoid!"

I had to buy a new shop! It was too many memories hunting me at the old bakery! Once people heard about what happened, business slowed down. When I went into a deep depression. I decided to close down for a while! As if that wasn't enough. Somebody burned it down. Of course, I knew Tasha and Carmen did it! My mother told me not to worry about it and that she'd handle it!

Two weeks later, some fishermen found two couples floating in the river! Tasha and Kevin Carman and Richard. Swept away in the current during a late-night boat ride! Funny! Richard never liked boat rides!

"I want you at that address tonight! I need to punish that pussy for the bad things it's been doing!" Sonny demanded with a smile and my kitty jumped!

"All of my instructions are in the invitation!" He acknowledged and vanished out the bakery doors!

I ran into my office to retrieve the invite! The envelope was off-white with a burgundy seal on the front. It read, Hats 6901 (BF) Cats Lane Blvd.

You need to be naked under your trench coat! Freshly waxed. Thigh-high boots only! Hair down and wear dark sunglasses. When you reach the basement, doors at 6pm knock five times. The password is cream! Don't be late or else!

Good thing I have a trench coat and thigh-high boots! I also got a fresh wax this morning! Yes! I couldn't get home fast enough! I brushed my teeth, showered, washed, and blow-dried my hair. I lotioned up with my new blueberry-lemon body cream!

I found my maroon trench coat in the back of the closet, still in the cleaner's bag! I zipped up my black thigh-highs in record time and was out the door by 5:30pm. Traffic was lite, so I knew I'd be there on time!

When I arrived at my destination. I almost thought I was at the wrong address because this is a high-class strip club. However, I remembered (BF) means the basement floor! Let me just take a breath! Once the big tall giant bodyguard opened the door, my sexual senses skyrocketed to fucking Mars!

Sonny stood before me with black leather pants and no shirt! Ahhh! His muscles have muscles! That V reminds me of Major's, I had to shake my head. Back to Sonny. "I see you followed instructions, and you smell nice too!" "Thank You!" I said nervously, walking down a long dark hallway.

"I think you're going to like what you see! If not, tell me, and I'll walk you out!" He assured. When we rounded the corner, my knees grew weak! There was an audience sitting in the middle of the room. They had dividers between tables, so you couldn't really see who was sitting next to you. There were several stages in each section with a sex swing or a massage table! Only we kept walking.

We entered a room with a bed and a pole! The pole had two handcuffs hooked on both sides, top and bottom. Me being a freak, I didn't utter a word. I was ready for whatever. He blindfolded me, and locked me up on the pole, and put nipple pinchers on me! I almost climaxed. Then he teased me over and over and over until a pain built up in my stomach!

Once he saw I had tears in my eyes, Sonny drummed the pain right out of me! Satisfied and spent! He snatched off the blindfold to reveal a whole room of people had been watching! Was I mad? Hell no! I wanted to do it again until I noticed the other people in the room next to us! That's Terry and English having a threesome with......

Chapter 12: Landin Forest

I am beyond stressed the fuck out! I haven't had any pussy in weeks. Sage is now a Lawyer herself, so finding an assistant that can match her work ethic is hard as hell! Sage promised she would find me an assistant last week, and I have yet to see the muthafucker! The case I'm working on has turned into a game of finding Nemo. And Kelly keeps texting me things she's added to an already long-ass birthday list! Hell, I still had a blanky at 4 years old, and that's all I cared about.

"Here are your cappuccino's, Sir!" The lovely lady at Chocolate Cup Coffee shop sang. Miss Alice always hooks me up with two cappuccinos. "You look tired young man!" "Miss Alice, I am exhausted, but the world still turns!" "Yes, it does. You have an altering task that will test your spirit. Be careful; it's deeper than you think! Her actions were taught," And with that, she left!

The last time Miss Alice said some cryptic shit like that to me. I almost went over to English's house to kill her ass! Kelly ran up to me after Sunday school crying! She said English told her not to eat any more donuts, or she was going to get fat. And that I will starve her because I don't like fat kids.

I mean, I got all the way to her driveway when Miss Alice's words resonated. *"A snake is going to bite you with hurtful words! The plan is to paint a false illusion to your loved ones."* When I tell you, I almost fucked up. Believe me! I looked towards English's window, and she was standing there naked! There is no telling what she had planned for me behind that door! Needless to say, English was removed from being the Sunday school teacher for the toddler's group!

I searched through a few files while sipping my cappuccino and couldn't help but laugh at the information before me! My client, Vina, is suing her ex-boyfriend for getting her fired from her dream job!

This fool thought she was cheating on him every time she left the house! He would sit in the parking lot of her place of business in different family member's cars. Whenever Vina and her co-workers went out for drinks, Pete would sit in the back of the restaurant and text her the whole time!

The second to last straw with Vina's boss was when he busted into a meeting, thinking she was sucking him off! He opened the door with so much force the papers on the conference table flew off! The last straw was when they had to work late. Vina's boss got a call from the security office saying someone was outside on the ground, trying to peer into the window!

At night it's hard to see out the window. So, Mr.Wills got a flashlight out of his desk. He then turned off the lights to the office and flashed the light on the window! For sure, as horse shit stinks. Pete was under the bushes, looking into the window like a creepy little crawler! Vina snapped pictures on her phone, which made significant evidence.

Mr. Wills promised to hire Vina back after the trial, so I told her not to worry. However, I think she would be a perfect fit for a position in Jaylin's security firm. As for Pete, that son of a bitch is worth $300 Million, and Vina only wants $300,000 for pain and suffering!

I gathered my things and headed to the office! "Hey! Mr. Forest, your new assistant, is waiting in your office with Mrs. Forest." Miss Kathy informed. "Thank you!" I headed to my office and almost turned around to ask Miss Kathy if I was human.

Sage knows I'm a man, and my weakness is women with big asses! Now don't get me wrong, my wife has the perfect ass. I wouldn't trade her for anything in the world. But who in their right mind! Would hire a woman with an ass like that to be around their husband?

"Hi baby, this is Emery, my replacement. She attended law school in Germany, but her parents relocated to the states! However, she moved here to help take care of them!" "I got this," Emery assured, putting her hand on Sage's shoulder! Sage has told me a lot about you and how you like things! I'm a quick learner, and I can and will do whatever you want me to!" Sex dripped right off of Emery's tongue, and my wife is sitting here, clueless as fuck!

Chapter 13: Kiley Banks

"**I** don't know why you keep buying those ugly white shoes for Ashley!"

My mom sighed as she handed me a box of white shoes she kept throwing away! "I'm trying to teach her a lesson! I don't want Ashley to agree when she really doesn't! I want her to speak and think for herself. Every time we go shopping, she agrees with everything I like to make me happy."

"Nanna C, can you tie my sneakers? Ut, Oh! Hi! Mom!"

"Oh, no, you don't, Ashley! You need to explain why you keep throwing your church shoes away?"

"I don't like them, Mommy, there so ugly, and they don't match with anything!" I had to laugh at her little face!

"From here on out, you need to speak up, okay?"

"Okay! Can I have those red sneakers I like for my Birthday?"

"Mabe!" She ran off to answer the door with my dad! He's her favorite because he lets her do whatever she wants! And that's why he has…."

"Do you know you have barrettes hanging from your beard! What the hell you and Celia got going on over here?" Grandfather Red asked, looking around like something was really going on.

"I did it, great Red Koolaid!" Ashely popped out from behind my dad! "I gave him a makeover! Come on so I can get started on yours!" I laughed because Red looked like he wanted to run back out the door.

"I came over here because I need yall to take Raymond's old ass, I mean butt! He is messing up my groove and Rose won't give me no…."

"Red!" My mom screeched.

"Candy! She won't give me any candy!" He corrected!

"Are you supposed to have candy, great Red?" Ashley asked.

"Yes, I'm supposed to have more than what I'm not getting!" I hit the floor! I don't know how Nanna Rose put up with this old man!

Today I'm going to teach my sister-in-laws' and Angel how

to use butterfly knives! My cousin Knightly customized them into barrette clips! Knightly is another cold asset to the Elite which, I'm sure will have her own story! I've never shown anyone besides my husband my Knife collection. So this should be fun!

"Hey!..."

I curled up in a fit of laughter! First of Angel and ILynn are wearing shiny long-sleeved black leotards with a black knife holster belt around their waist. Sage wore a full army fatigue catsuit with a drop-leg holster belt!

"We ready to slice and dice some shit!" Angel said.

I led the girls to my closet and hit a few buttons. The wall split open, and my shelves rotated into position! The look on their faces was priceless!

"Now choose which one yall wanna work with first! Sage and Angel wanted the butterfly knives while ILynn picked the samurai! My girl! With her weak stomach having ass! "Let's go to my she shed, Sherrals!" We all laughed!

"I know one thing and two things for sure this is not a regular she shed!!! This is one of Dexter's kill rooms! "ILynn replied nervously.

I sat two cantaloupes and three watermelons, each on their

chopping blocks.

"It's all about upper strength and quick thinking. Now ILynn, I want you to slice the watermelons." Her form was perfect, but she thought too long and hard, and that's why it didn't go all the way through.

"What's up, Sage? You just checked out on me. You good?"

"Yeah, I'm just thinking about a case." She lied.

"I can always tell when she lies because her left eye twitches!

"Okay, I'll let that one go this time!" I laughed.

"Do any of you think I rushed Landin into marriage?" She asked, on the verge of tears!

"Are you kidding? I mean, everybody knows you can't rush that nigga into shit!" ILynn assured.

I thought it was a bit rushed, but who am I to speak on it! Sage always threatened Landin about dating other people if he didn't decide.

"Well, I guess he didn't want anybody else to have you! I said sarcastically.

"Did something happen to where you feel like you rushed into marriage?" Angel asked.

"I just want him to be sure he wanted marriage and not to please me.

I'm testing his love for me! I just need to be sure!" I was about to ask her what she meant, but her phone rang! I'm just going to mind my business for now.

Chapter 14: Ashton Banks

hat the fuck do you mean the power went out, and the backup generator wasn't working?"

Kyle was sitting at my desk with his pods on! While Terry tried to explain why we couldn't catch the person who swiped money out of our account! First, we have top-of-the-line security equipment in this bank. Second, someone would have had to cut the generator off because it's run by a battery. Third I can spot a lie before it's spoken!

"Did you steal from our accounts?" Christian calmly asked.

"No, I already told you I wouldn't do that!" Terry pleaded, trying desperately to control the vein dying to pop out of her forehead.

"Listen, Terry, if I find out you did this, I'm going to cut off all of your fingers! I dismissed her, and she all but ran out of the room.

"Bruh, she was lying through her spaced teeth!" Christian

commented.

"The vein in her forehead almost burst! Bella is up to something. Just think about it. When the will was read, and the Lawyer announced our equal shares. She flipped. I'm telling you, Bella is behind this!

Major told me he found the offshore account in Switzerland, but of course, the cameras weren't working. I told you not to hire her, Ashton! As conniving as she was all through high school. Did you really think she'd changed?"

Damn, he's mad as hell. "I didn't think her behavior in the past would affect her skill here at the bank. I didn't realize how much distress Terry was causing you, Christian." I answered honestly

"Now, you wanna be a smart ass about it. Knowing damn well, if I hired Iesha's crazy-ass without consulting with you first, you would've been trying to fight, Ashton!"

I had to spit my drink out at the mention of my ex! If Christian only knew what happened to Iesha a few months ago, he wouldn't have mentioned her name!

"Well, it would be pretty hard for her to do an interview." I laughed.

"What are you talking about nigga?" Christian asked.

"You know that underground sex dungeon nobody is supposed to know about?" I asked.

"Yeah, please don't tell me you and Kiley went to that shit!" Christian chuckled.

"We were extended an invitation from one of Kiley's coworkers, and I thought why not since I was curious about the whole Fifty Shades of Gray craze. Bruh! It was some freaky shit going on down there! They had open rooms and stages where people could watch you have sex.

It was a thick-ass chocolate girl suspended in mid-air doing the splits. While two niggas were feasting on her like she was the last chocolate moon pie! Then there were two more thick chicks on their knees, deep throating the dudes.

"Really nigga!" Christian's eyes almost popped out.

"Hold on, I'm not finished! This shit went on forever!The chicks on the ground were sitting on two guys' faces while two other thick hotties were riding the dudes with cowboy hats on! I promise I'm not making this shit up!"

"What kind of chain smokin orgy was this? Did yall crazy asses put on a show?" Christian asked.

"No, we had a private room in which I'm grateful for what I'm about to tell you! We'd just finished an intense round with

Kiley in the swing!"

"TMI!" Christian chimed.

"She thought it would be fun to tie me up and use a whip! Only you have to go and purchase such items in another private area! Kiley left me tied up and blindfolded while she left the room.

It seemed like she'd been gone for thirty minutes when I felt her put me in her mouth! Only, I knew something was wrong when I heard gagging noises! The cloth over my eyes was thin, so I moved it up with ease using my arm. Nigga I started bucking like a horse to kick that bitch off of me! But my feet were also tied.

Iesha thought it was funny, so every time I bucked, she sucked. She says, "I knew that was you! I had Jamal take his time finding what your wife requested. I just wanted to taste why you left me! Umm! She's delectable!" Then she started teasing me by swirling her long tongue around the head.

I'd just popped my hand out of the cuffs! When Kiley came in and snatched Iesha's tongue right out her mouth! That muthafucker hit the wall with a thud I'll never forget!"

"I'm surprised she didn't cut your dick off, but then again, it wasn't your fault!" Kiley's Auntie B said from the doorway!

Needless to say, she caught both Christian and me off guard as she appeared out of nowhere!

"Hey, Auntie B, What brings you to our neck of the woods!" I asked.

"Oh, I was just coming to relieve you of Kyle. Kiley told me you brought him to work with you! I figured I'd take all my great-nieces and nephews shopping for their upcoming birthdays!"

Shit! I jumped up and printed out two long lists of shit! Hell, we got twins!

"Oh, and I'm going to need you to write down the address to that place you were talking about. That freaky shit you saw got me all hot and bothered!" We all laughed as she and Kyle walked out the door.

"We have some spoiled ass kids!" Christian commented.

Knock! Knock! Christian and I both turned towards the door, a little startled,

"Hey! Doctor Bradley, how can we help you?"

"I apologize for barging in on you two, but this is an urgent matter. I've been looking into your grandparents' autopsy reports. They didn't die of natural causes. They were both poisoned! Who was in charge of administering their meds?" Dr.

Bradley fretted, concerned.

"Bella!" Christian and I shouted in unison!

That bitch!

Chapter 15: Terry

Me: Bella, you need to call me asap! I think they're on to us bitch!

Bella: Stop, Terry, you're paranoid!

Me: Call me paranoid all you want, but they questioned me about the backup generator. When I was with Christian, he could always tell when I lied. He would give me that look of disgust! Bella, you need to put the money back!

Bella: I'm not putting shit back. That money belongs to me! Stop texting me! You're supposed to be finessing Christian.

I don't know why I let Bella get me roped into this shit! I was doing just fine, finessing old men to pay for my expensive lifestyle. Of course, I could pay for it myself, but why when having a body like this! Men fall all over my double Ds and bouncy ass! However, the only man I want is married and not paying me the slightest bit of attention.

"Did you get in trouble?" My annoying young assistant

asked.

"No, don't you have some accounts to look over?" Jeez, she is always in my business! She needs to go take some Instagram pictures or something! Ol' Fashion Nova Queen!

"It didn't look that way to me. You were sitting in that chair shaking in your boots!" Cassie cackled. This bitch!

"I see his tongue lashing still has you in a daze so, I'll just go back to my desk."

"Yes, that will be a great idea! Thank You!" I walked to the bathroom so I could get myself together! Cassie was right. I was definitely shaken into almost confessing! They'll probably fire me, and the good Lord knows I don't need that stain on my perfect record.

Bella and I were considered attention whores in school! On the other hand, Bella had a sweet way of hiding it, but it was there. It only grew into a monster when we reached our senior year! All the guys wanted a taste of Bella and me. We were both 5'7 with perky double Ds and colossal asses, giving us the nickname double chocolate twins!

I was in love with Christian Banks, and I would stop at nothing to get him to notice me! It didn't really take much, and when I finally got him. I got comfortable thinking he was sprung on my sexy looks.

He started showing interest in another hottie named Felicia! This girl was 5'5 chocolate with long wavy hair! She must have been half Indian! Christian would drool and gawk at her huge ass that seemed to take up a lot of space in his big ass head!

A few weeks after walking Felicia to class, Christian totally forgot about me! The calls stopped and eating with me at lunch stopped. Over the weekend, I thought maybe if I gave him some pussy! He would forget all about little miss thickness. It worked for all of two months, then he was right back under Felicia's ass!

Bella, however, caught the eye of Jaylin Forest. He would come and pick Kiley and Landin up from school. She would make it a habit to be outside just so she could get a peek. At the time, it was rumored Jaylin was dating Bella's rival, Jessica.

Jessica was chocolate with green eyes, and that drove Bella crazy. Bella used to wear green contacts hoping to get more attention from Jaylin. Well, for a while, it worked until it didn't. Jaylin just disappeared, and the scheming lying Bella was born. I even followed her lead and regretted it to this day!

I told Christian that my step-father had been trying to

force himself on me for months and that I was afraid he would succeed. However, what i wasn't expecting was for him to call me out on my bullshit. Turns out Christain's father and my stepfather had been away on business for months. Needless, to say, he stopped fucking with me.

∞∞∞

Looking at Christian from my desk only made me hotter! I can only imagine how his grown dick could handle me. Snap! Snap! Snap! The sound of Christian's fingers brought me out of my lust-filled daydream.

"We don't pay you to daydream, Terry!"

"I'm sorry, do you need anything?" I desperately wanted him to need me.

"Yeah, I need you in my office right now!" He said as he turned and swiftly walked back to his office. I jumped up full of hope! I reached in my purse and grabbed my feminine spray to freshen up the kitty! I walked into his office, prepared to spread my legs for him on his desk!

When I stepped into his office Christian was sitting behind his desk, unbuttoning his suit jacket.

"Have a seat."

"Where?" I said in a flirtatious tone.

"In the fucking chair! Where else?" Christian spat.

"Listen, Terry, you need to keep it all the way professional when dealing with me. I have a wife and son that I will not jeopardize for a piece of ass! So, stop with the flirting and hicking up your skirt to show your twat!" I just shook my head because he just killed my thumping music.

"Did Bella ever ask you to check on my Grandparents? I mean, with you living next door to them." Christian asked, concerned.

"Yes, Bella would drop off their med packs on Thursdays and Fridays, and I would administer them. Which was weird because they had their own meds on their nightstands." Christian just sat there for what seemed like forever before he told me I was dismissed.

As I sat behind my desk, thinking back on those times, she asked me to help her out with her grandparents. I got angry. First, Bella comes up with this elaborate plan to seduce Christian. Now I'm being questioned about meds. Naw! Bella wouldn't have dared harmed her grandparents. Would she? And if so, did this bitch set me up?

BJ: Come sit on my face!

Me: Where is Bella? I thought she was sitting on your face earlier.

BJ: She was, but she had to go home to Hubby, And besides, I want some more chocolate ice cream!

Me: I'm on my way!

Yes, I'm fucking with BJ's fine ass every chance I get! His money is long, and he's excellent with his tongue! At least to me, he is!

Chapter 16: Major Forest

"Y all need to meet me over dad's house ASAP!" I said into my brother's home PA system!

I knew it was rude as fuck, but the tone in my dad's voice was more than urgent. Anytime I have to hop out the gushy on some bullshit! I get really fucking frustrated. That's the side of me everyone hates. So, I need whatever this announcement is to be laid out quickly. So, I can dive back into ILynn's ocean!

"Good Evening, Sons. I just found out some disturbing news. The white wolf has been shopping around for judges to pay off, and as of late, it's come to my attention that he's found one!" My father sighed.

"What are his claims?" Landin asked. "He claims there was an original will, in which we all know there wasn't.

The one and only will contains all of the original members of the Thee Elite on it. It's a non-contestable will. All of the land willed to us is ours and ours alone."

"He must've presented them with some kind of document," Landin said.

Dad handed him the papers he was served. Landin started laughing, which eased my mood a little bit. Because I was ready to go and kill somebody.

"This is fake! He must really have something on the Judge who pushed this through! This will is dated the year after Billy Sr's. Death! This should have been thrown out immediately."

"Good work, son! Major, I need you to find all incriminating evidence that little bastard has on the Judge. And Jaylin, we need to have 24hr surveillance on the white wolf."

"Already on it," Jaylin replied.

Something was off with Jaylin, his mien was marinating in regret, and his eyes were void of happiness.

"I'm good nigga!" Jaylin spat!

I forgot his ass is a mind reader!

"You don't look like your good!" Landin countered. Jaylin sighed while typing on his laptop. "I might have to kill my wife!"

"What?" Landin yelped as he stopped taking the phone from his ear.

"Bella's been moving funny! Things I should have picked up on a long time ago are now drilling a hole into my mind. I've been beating myself up over this shit!"

"Have you thought about counseling?" Our father asked.

"We're way past getting help, dad! Bella changed after she had Jr.

It's as though she became jealous of her own child. Christian and Ashton said they tried to warn me about her being an attention freak. Either I didn't see it or didn't want to. I can't deny the shit now, though." I stood up to give my brother a hug because he never shared his problems. You wouldn't know anything until that person was pushing up daisies.

"Does anybody know when Auntie B is bringing our kids home!" Landin asked.

"Shit! She's probably teaching them how to make eyeball necklaces!" Dad remarked nonchalantly.

It took us a few seconds to let what Rumond said sink in before the three of us jumped up and headed for the door!

Chapter 17: Auntie B (Aunt Bobbye)

"**T**his is so much fun! My mommy is going to love this necklace and bracelet!" May-Lynn chirped.

"Mine too! Kelly and Ashley agreed.

Jr. and CJ made caterpillar key chains! Which looked totally awesome! I love spending time with my great-nieces and nephews. Growing up for me at this age was hard! We learned quickly that the world was evil because nothing was hidden from us.

I always wanted to be like Red because he was strong and smart! Some parents told their kids to be quiet, never look white people in the eye, and say anything clever!

Not our parents. We would get our asses whooped if we didn't look everybody in their eyes. We were taught how to respond quickly and sharply! Cut them with your words, my momma used to say!

The older I got, the bolder people began to try me! After Victorious's sister and her babies were murdered. Our lives changed. I was sixteen at the time when I noticed the changes in my body. I had the shape of a grown woman, and some old nasty perverted white men took notice. I don't know what made me take a shortcut from school. There was an alleyway behind our house, and at the end of it stood a group of men.

As soon as they spotted me, they immediately headed in my direction. I took off running, but what I saw at the other end of the alley made me more afraid of the guys chasing me. There stood my father with black eyes and bulging veins coming out of his neck! I'd never seen so much blood in my life! I was so mesmerized I couldn't turn away! He'd ripped those men to pieces!

The training was gruesome and extensive, but I never complained, not once. The more I walked the earth with racism in my face, the more eager I'd become to shut them down. I know that's not why I was trained, but it's where my mind lived.

A year later, it was time for me to graduate high school! I was so excited my mom let me go shopping for a new dress. My favorite color is green. I don't know why I was drawn to that color, but it was beautiful against my skin tone. As we entered the dress store, a white girl in my class rushed over to hug me! Everybody in the store could see how pissed her dad was that she touched a Negro girl. He made her change her clothes and wash herself down in the restroom. Jennifer cried the whole time, telling me how sorry she was.

The only thing I noticed out of the whole situation was Jennifer's dad had green eyes! So, the night after graduation, I followed him to one of those racy film rooms. He was so focused on naked women that he didn't see me standing in front of him until it was too late. I snatched out both of his green eyes and took off running! That was the beginning of my madness!

I had a list of assholes who called me a little black bitch, a black nigger girl, or a monkey. Jennifer even showed me where some of them lived. Needless to say, her dad died from his injuries, leaving Jennifer and her abused mother very wealthy! Due to both of Mr. Washington's eyes missing, he ran out into the middle of the street, where he was smashed like a pancake.

Unfortunately, my spree didn't stop there after being seen running away with eyeballs in my hand. My father sent me out to live with my Aunt in California. Do you know how many green-eyed men walked around in Cali? A whole fucking lot!

I don't know what Raymond thought his sister was going to do. Hell, she started helping me! Aunt Raina was a jewelry maker. Therefore, she taught me everything about turning my collection into shiny new jewels.

BOOM! BOOM! BOOM! Who the hell is beating on my door like that!

"Where the kids at....Aww! Hell, we're too late!" Major blasted, barging his way through the door.

"Aww! Auntie, you got our kids wearing human remains around their necks and wrist. What the hell are those keychains?" Landin asked.

"I soaked them in resin and painted them. You can't even tell, so shut the hell up before you scare my babies!" I spat, checking to see if they heard our conversation.

"Look! Daddy, I made you and mommy gold chains!"

While they gathered the kids, my husband walked out to greet everyone! They hadn't seen him in years.

Dom is a private contractor and doesn't get to travel with me as much. I know they're wondering why his appearance is a little different. And no, I don't feel like explaining right now!

"Uncle, What happened to your eye? Landin's nosey ass asked. That's when I noticed everyone staring at me. Why did his pirate eye-looking ass have to come out here? Damn!

Chapter 18: Bella Forest

I f I had it my way, I would build a man. I would keep my husband's body but change his attention span and his huge 13-inch dick for BJ's comfortable size 71/2. BJ can't get enough of me. I hated I had to hop off his face, but my duties been lacking, and I refused to let another bitch step in my place.

Jaylin called me saying I needed to come and pick Jr. up from his job because he had an emergency interview! Who the hell has an emergency interview?

"Hey! Allen is Jaylin in his office?" I asked, headed in that direction.

"Uh, he's in an interview right now...." I burst right through the office door, not giving a fuck about who was on the other side.

The sight before me made me instantly sick to my stomach! There was this medium brown-skinned Teyana Taylor Look-alike with a pixy cut made perfect for her face. Her lips were to die for, and I'm not even going to describe her body! You'll jump off a bridge. The worse part is these muthafuckas have yet to acknowledge my presence! Not even my own son!

The stars in my husband's eyes while looking at her are breaking my heart. I haven't seen that sparkle in years!

"I'm sorry, Mr. Forest, I told Mrs. Forest you were conducting an interview." Ol snitching ass Allen blabbed out of breath.

"It's fine, Allen. Go get your bag and go with your mother, Jr.," Jalin instructed.

"Aww! Do I have to go with mommy? I wanna stay here and talk to Miss Vina!"

Oh, hell, naw! "What time will you be home for dinner, Jaylin!" I asked with a pissy attitude.

"We already ate dinner, mommy!" That's when I saw the takeout boxes from Las Alamedas, my favorite fucking restaurant.

"Since when do you host dinner for job interviews?" I looked at him to miss popular.

"Since it took you an hour and a half to pick up our son!" Jaylin responded void any life for me in his eyes.

I did take my time getting here because I wanted to see

what Terry was talking about. Only she'd left work early. She could be a pain in the ass, but I need her as my scapegoat!

"So, you just assumed I wouldn't make dinner for my HUSBAND AND SON?" I emphasized.

"I'm sorry, Vina. Can you excuse us for a second?" He gently asked her.

This bitch had to be an inch taller than me with longbow legs. As her scent made its way into my nostrils, I became angrier. Thoughts of her being able to handle Jaylin's immense tool flashed across my mind! There is no way I'm letting this bitch take my man. After Vina and my son left the room, Jaylin just stood there and peered into my eyes, laced with secrets.

"Why aren't your lips moving? It seems you had a lot to say when Vina was in here. You out here pretending to be wife and mother of the fucking year. My son and I haven't had your cooking in months. Thanks to Major, mom, and myself. We've been doing just fine without your concern about meals." I looked toward the door because Jaylin's voice was a little elevated than usual.

"Don't worry, she can't hear me since that's your only concern. Now, if you will excuse me. I need to finish briefing my new assistant on her duties!"

"Your assistant? What the fuck, Jaylin? You must think I'm stupid! Since when did you need any assistance with your work!" I spat.

"Did you, or did you not say I work too much?"

I couldn't say shit! I just headed towards the door. Before I could reach the handle, Jaylin said, "Strike two!"

"What the hell is that supposed to mean, Jaylin?" "It means you're fucking up!"

"Whatever, don't fucking threaten me!"

Jaylin dropped an envelope with his security firm information on it! "You seriously think you can leave all of this ass I'm throwing!" I bent over in front of him, picked the envelope up, and stuffed it in my handbag.

"You can barely do that!" Jaylin said under his breath, but I heard him!

On our way home, I decided to make a detour back to BJ's. Jr. was asleep, so I left him in the car. I could have sworn I saw Terry's white BMW Sedan pulling off of this street! I found the spare key under the mat! I eased inside just in case he was sleeping.

"Aye! What the hell? I could have stabbed you with this toothbrush!" BJ yelped. BJ is half-nacked and brushing his teeth in the middle of the day!

"Who was here other than me today, BJ?" "Nobody, why?" I thought I saw Terry leave from over here! Are you fucking her, too, BJ?" i asked getting pissed off

"If I was, I don't need your permission to do it!"

"You better not be fucking on, Terry!"

"Man, go on with that bullshit, Bella! You have a whole husband you should probably go home to. I'm tired as fuck and need to get some sleep." I turned to leave, but BJ grabbed me by my hair and bit my neck!"

"Are you out of your mind, BJ? Jaylin is going to kill me if you left a mark!" I fussed in a panic.

Six months after dating BJ, he started asking questions about Jaylin. I didn't think anything of it as I was enjoying my newfound sexual liberation. BJ drove my ego to heights unknown!

I loved how he yelled my name and moaned out like a bitch.

That's what I wanted my husband to do! I know I'm not satisfying Jaylin, but it should be all about me. I'm the most critical person in this relationship. Happy wife, happy life, right? Oh, fuck I just remembered Jr being in the car by himself.

I caught a chill on the back of my neck as I neared my car. There was another vase of beautiful wildflowers. What the hell is going on with the stupid courier! Why the hell isn't there a note! I reached in my purse for my keys and pulled out the envelope I swiped from Jaylin.

It was a bunch of documents I didn't care to read. But the one that stood out to me the most was the one with dollar signs! $4.5 Billion I didn't even read the rest! I signed my name under Jaylin's and mailed it off to the address written on the front! I could have orgasmed right there at the thought of being part-owner of a multi Billion dollar company$$$

Chapter 19: JLynn Forest

"These grandkids are spoiled as hell! I remember throwing yall parties in the backyard, not trickin out big ass warehouses!"

We are currently looking for materials to build a chocolate layer for our five-year-olds. I was thinking of a candy crush floor with chocolate stations set up throughout the warehouse.

There will be a couple chocolate fountains at each table, however. MayLynn and Kelly are healthy kids that don't eat candy. I have a unique table with veggies, fruit smoothies, and slushies!

"We might as well keep this shit open for the public. This is a cash cow if you ask me!" Grandfather Victor Sr. estimated.

"Look at you, thinking of a bigger picture!" We both laughed!

I want all the rides on one side of the room. That way, we

can keep an eye out for all the children at once. The physical games will be performed in the middle of the floor. We're also going to have an event for adults. We all have to wear all white, and whoever comes out of the whole party clean. Will receive $1,500!

"I know what else is a cow!" My grandmother Elenore aired, walking towards us. "Don't come in here with all that shit, Ella. This is a happy place for the grandkids!" He pressed. "You make sure you keep that same energy when you tell Linda you can't find her a house! I mean it, Vic! If I see you out on another lunch date with that homewrecker! I'm gonna snatch ya balls off!" Grandmother declared.

Grandfather sighed for what seemed like five whole minutes while I held my breath to keep from laughing! "You better suck some air into your lungs, or ya old ass is gonna pass out fuckin with me!" And with that, she left! I know I'm not supposed to get into their business. And I'm trying hard not to ask, but the suspense is killing me!

"Yo, grandma is crazy! I was having lunch by my damn self when my ex, Linda, and her double-wide hips, invited herself to have a seat at my table! She started talking about how she heard I was doing great with my real estate business! She asked me for my services when Elenore walked in with a ball of fire behind her."

I just sat there with my mouth hung low! I've never in my years of living seen her get that mad at grandfather. "I mean, I don't know why Linda came back here. Elenore beat that woman within an inch of her life 35 years ago! I'll never forget the hurt in Ella's eyes." he confessed

Well, what happened?" I asked anxiously! "It's a bit graphic, so bear with me, young buck! It was after Red won an incredibly tricky case. The trial took months and was putting wear and tear on his mental! When Red won the case by a confession on the stand! He wanted to have a small celebratory dinner!

Ella and I would randomly go have sex in a room, closet, or car! I guess you can say your grandmother and I were very spontaneous creatures! In the middle of the party, I'd gone to the restroom. When I came out, there was a note on the door telling me to go to the guest room right across from the bathroom. The letter also said not to turn on the light!

It happened so quickly! Once I closed the room door, my pants were pulled down! I was receiving the ride of my life when Ella burst into the room!" "How did she know you were in that room!" I curiously asked. "I must've dropped the note in the hallway. Ella cut the light on, and I froze dead in my tracks. Linda tried to jump off of me to run, but she was too slow.

Ella struck Linda so hard you could hear Linda's nose break! However, Ella didn't stop there. She broke both of Linda's legs and fractured her ribs. Ella then whispered in Linda's ear, telling her once she heals, she better move far away from the South as possible!

"Wow! How long did it take for her to forgive you even though it really wasn't your fault?" "Shit! Ella didn't talk to me for months! She said I should have been able to feel that it wasn't her! I could agree, but it was pitch black in that room! All my brain registered was me being in something wet and gushy!" "TMI! Grandfather!" It's hilarious hearing my Grandparents use slang from rap songs!

The contractors gave us their word on completing the task by Thursday. We'll do a run-through on Friday and set everything in its position for the party on Saturday! I didn't have to buy any presents for MayLynn, because Auntie B bought everything on all of the kids' lists! I didn't say anything because the look in her eyes said not to! I simply thanked her and went on about my day!

"Hey, can you come by the shop on your way home? I need to show you something!" Angel demanded!

"Sure, just let me finish up the gift bags for MayLynns Tai Kwon Do class.

Imagine my surprise when I saw Serta, one of Major's many fuck buddies, come strolling through Tai Kwon Do class yesterday. Mind you, I hadn't seen this bitch not once since before the invitations went out!

Serta was inappropriately dressed to be around little kids, but I guess she figured she'd try her luck on seeing Major here. When she spoke, I immediately knew she was about to be on some bullshit.

"Is Major aware of me coming to the party?

I don't want there to be any issues." She asked, grinning from ear to ear.

"Why would it be an issue, Serta?"

"You know because he and I fuck every now and then." I just giggled.

"You mean used to fuck?"

"That's what I said, ILynn. Used to fuck." She chuckled.

I simply reminded her that this would be a party for children and to dress appropriately! She tried to talk, but I kept it cute and went on about my day.

Serta is one of those parents to send the grandparent in to do her job, or she'll drop her off and pick her up, not wanting to be bothered. It's funny how the memory of a good dick makes you show your ass! She tried it, though! I know clearly Major wouldn't fuck it all up for somebody like Serta.

∞ ∞ ∞

"What's up? You had an urgency in your voice!" I asked while looking at what possibly could be the problem. There Serta and three guys sat waiting for service. I don't even know how to describe the country backwood niggas she had with her! All I know is if they start some shit. They're gonna get this butterfly clip jabbed through their throats.

"Girl, this bitch came in here trying to play nice like I don't remember her talking all that shit about me beating her cousin's ass and making her disappear. She better watch out before I have Caleb braid her brains out of her scalp! It's not my fault; her cousin lost her head!" We both laughed.

"Did you get everything on MayLynns list?" She quizzed.

"No, Auntie B did!"

"What! I'm about to send her CJ's long-ass list right now! She got six months!" I turned to look at Serta, and she was having an in-depth conversation with one of the guys she was with! I'm going to have to keep my eye on this bitch.

Ping! I looked at my phone, and there was a text message from an unknown number that read: When the hats lurk, the kitties twerk! 69.

"Why is your lip turned?" Angel questioned. I showed her my phone, and she showed me hers!

"What the fuck is this?"

Chapter 20: Sage Forest

I almost gave in to my husband's advances this morning! I wanted nothing more than to drive that diesel till noon! I know you all think I'm a fool, but I can't get what happened to my Aunt out of my mind. She agreed to marry Donald six months after meeting him. Three months after dating. Donald mentioned his sister's best friend needing a place to stay while her house was being built.

Aunt Cree didn't pay it any mind until he asked her if she preferred his quest lived elsewhere. Donald didn't want her to be uncomfortable about her staying there. Just to show Aunt Cree his loyalty! Donald had given her a key to use whenever she pleased. Of course, aunt Cree told him no. She believed he wouldn't do anything to jeopardize their relationship.

Having temptation around and not giving in to it solidifies their love. So she thought! I guess her intuition starting fucking with her, so she started withholding sex and using working late as an excuse not to see him. Eager to know the outcome of her plan. Aunt Cree decided to use her key at a time;

she knew he would be asleep!

Slipping into his house was simple, and depending on the outcome, she was going to break his back in with what she was keeping him from. As she neared his bedroom door, she heard shuffling and slurping noises. Aunt Cree opened the door, and Donald and temptation were in a full 69 position, feasting on each other like it was their last desert!

Unlike many women scorned, Aunt Cree didn't wallow in pain. She jumped on the next train and kept it moving! Donald couldn't take her moving on so quickly, so he killed her and then himself. I was devastated, but thanks to Mrs. Forest, I survived!

With all of that on my brain, I feel that testing my husband is very necessary! I need to know I didn't marry too quickly and that he got his whorish ways out of his system. I know I gave Landin an ultimatum, and I shouldn't have. I regret doing so every day! I never wanted to force anyone to marry me.

I was sitting in the coffee shop when this beautiful girl walked up to my table. She asked if I minded her sitting with me since there weren't any more tables. She introduced herself as Emery, a Law student from Germany. Her parents fell on hard times and moved here to America. Emery admitted needing some fast money so, she strips part-time.

I remember thinking about how perfect she was for the job. I'm not saying I don't have a banging body. It's just that Landin is an ass man, and Emery has ass for days, weeks and months. She is a real test of the times! I put hidden cameras in his office and car! Yesterday when I viewed his office cam. He was staring at Emery's ass like it was a brand new shiny car! It hurt like hell, but he's a man, and that's what they do! As long as he doesn't touch it! He's free to look all he wants.

Emery seemed a little eager to get started, but I had to remind her what the job entails. Kissing and touching is cheating, and if he does, either it's over! I could tell the other day Kiley wanted to say something about pressuring Landin into marrying me! I'm sure he's shared with her the threats I made to him.

Grateful, she's been keeping to her word about not butting into our marriage. Kiley doesn't play about her brothers! I just hope she never catches wind of the crazy shit I'm doing. Yes, I could just ask him outright, but I feel like he'll just lie to keep me. I believe he loves me with his heart and soul! I just need to know he won't cheat when tested.

"Hey, girl, sorry it took so long. Your husband had me in his office taking notes!" Emery is dressed rather provocatively for work, but that's a part of the plan.

"How much longer do you want to do this? He's not taking the bait, I mean, he looks at my ass, but he won't touch it or get close to it." Emery observed.

"We have a lawyers convention next week and will need you as an assistant to tag along. We can up the advances then. I'll get adjoining rooms where you'll be lying in his bed when he arrives." The stars in her eyes did go unnoticed,

"Emery, by all means, you are NOT supposed to sleep with my husband! If he kisses or touches you anywhere on your body! Call it off, and I'll walk in and hand him divorce papers."

"Damn, do you really think he'll cheat on you; you're fucking beautiful, Sage. You are bright, well put together, and you don't have any extra bullshit behind you! I mean, even if he did cheat on you with me. Do you actually think he would leave you for me! I don't think so!" Emery grilled.

"Maybe if he knows he won't get caught, he'll take the bait!" I said, ignoring Emery's concerning glare.

It will be challenging to hide cameras in the hotel room, so I'll have to rely on your safe word.

"How about when he touches me? I'll moan out really loud." She suggested, biting her bottom lip!

"Perfect! I'll wire you the other half of the money in your

account tomorrow!" And with that, she left with a pep in her step!

Uh! Yes, I need a cappuccino to go, please! I spoke to the young cashier behind the counter of Chocolate Cup Coffee Shop! Landin and I discovered this coffee shop a few years ago, taking a walk downtown! The blueberry banana crunch muffin is to die for!

I sat down in the to-go area when a lovely lady brought me my cappuccino. She put her hand on my shoulder and said: "Sometimes actions you cause can never be fixed. Love has already been proven! Take caution, baby girl." I'm Miss Alice.

"Okay, nice to meet you, Alice." Her words prickled my skin. That was weird.

Chapter 21: Emery

I've made some easy money over the years doing side jobs with the scorned duo I call my handlers. My life wasn't all that great in Germany. Yes, I was in Law school with a bright future ahead. My parents worked really hard, and my brother worked harder to keep me in school. The problem was I broke up my professor's marriage. His wife had it in for me and wouldn't stop threatening me!

Mrs. Orich went to the dean and showed him video footage of us having sex all over the lecture hall after hours. Needless to say, I was kicked out of law school while he was placed on administrative leave for six weeks. I couldn't tell my family what happened. So, running into my handlers was a lifesaver if you asked me!

They brought me to America to get close to a few marks using my sex appeal. We would spend a lot of time in this high-class strip club. One night I had one too many drinks, which encouraged me to get on stage. I guess you can say I was a natural pole dancer because I effortlessly climbed and twirled around it like I was the headliner in a Vagas show!

Once I finished, I had so much money lying at my feet and men's tongues hanging out of their mouths. I don't know when I took off my clothes, but I was completely naked. After counting out the money I made, I decided that this was what I wanted to do! I made $20,000 in one night for doing a five-minute dance! The next night I made double. Who knew my bouncy voluptuous ass would make men tremble, fall to their knees, and give me all their cash.

My handlers noticed how excited money made me and offered me another opportunity to triple what I was making. They introduced me to the mysterious sex world downstairs and that's where the real money was! I wanted to start that night, but they had other plans.

They wanted me to get close to a guy named Christian. I still had a heavy accent, so I had to practice my English day and night! They thought I'd have a chance at being his new lady since he'd broken up with his girlfriend! Once I conquered his heart, I was to acquire about his family business! Although that never happened. Because he dismissed me like a plate of burnt cookies!

After receiving the underworld rules, my handlers and I decided to watch a very explicit show. In watching the show, we all became sexually enticed and started to touch on each other! Despite the fact, my female handler and I have never been with the same sex. The ambiance and attention we possessed washed away all doubt.

Our meetings became more frequent and more exhilarating than the last. Life seemed to be going great until the group's male counterpart wanted to add more spiders to an already webbed situation. Once he did that, the original female of the crew and I fell by the wayside!

The OG thought it best to branch out to do our own thing! But first, she suggested lightening my skin. The guy she wanted me to approach next was Christian's friend. So, altering my appearance will lessen the chances of getting caught! I told her Christian barely looked at my face because my ass had him hypnotized! He probably won't remember my face.

It took almost 2 years for my skin to completely lighten up! It used to be a beautiful dark chocolate Hershey bar to a medium tan golden pie crust. The only places that didn't lighten up are a few of my cuticles and my upper left but cheek! I just told people it was a birthmark. Because of the dark patch on my butt, I had to have my dance out-fits made uniquely to cover it!

I thought about getting a tattoo of a big ass Hersey bar to disguise it since it's the same shape. OG told me I needed to decide fast because moving forward to the next mark needed to happen quickly! She came up with a seductive plan to meet Landin at the coffee shop and pretend to need a house in the area. OG told me his now-wife took her home off the market, and she was 100% sure he didn't know about it!

I just needed to acquire about the home and mention the seller changed her mind. OG said to make sure my ass is the number one feature of the damsel in distress act. Only I didn't have to do any of that because I'd met his wife. She was fucking radiant! I never wanted to deviate from the plan, but I couldn't help myself.

I had to know about her, and just maybe she would be-friend me, so I could get closer to her husband that way. On the outside looking in, they had the perfect marriage. Hell! I ad-mittedly tried to reason with her, but the dollar signs coming from both sides made me submit. OG wasn't happy at first, but after giving it much thought. She deemed it a genius plan.

∞∞∞

Listening to Landin make plans to link up with his brothers gave me an idea! Maybe I could give him a story to tell them when they meet. I ran to the restroom to freshen up. I sprayed a little of Beyonce's heat seduction perfume on my neck, wrist, and between my thighs. I didn't care about the rule not to actually sleep with Landin. Let's be honest if the act presents itself, I'm surely going to hop on!

I stepped closer to him to make sure he inhaled my perfume. I then leaned over to pick up the paper clip I dropped earlier. I heard him suck in the air, letting me know I have right where I want him.

"Excuse me," I teased.

"Did you take a bath this morning? Something smells bad!" Landin complained.

Did this fool just say I smell?

Chapter 22: Jaylin Forest

I used to love how Bella woke me up with sloppy toppy after a disagreement. It was her way of saying she was sorry without saying it.

"Mmmmmmmmmmm! She hummed on my dick. "Do you like that, Jay?"

I observantly stared Bella in the eyes. Her body was telling me everything I needed to know. **One**, she's been practicing being as the tip of my stick is in her throat. She's never been able to do that.

Two, she swallowed the fruits of her labor, and I tried hard not to moan out like a bitch. She's never done that before, either. She must have taken my intense staredown as momentum to ride me! Fuck she was tight as she only allowed seven inches of me inside. I had six more inches to go, so I lifted up to get there.

What pissed me off is I broke a barrier that wasn't there before. I consider myself a patient man, but there is no return point when my heart is broken. I pushed up again, and you would have thought she had a painful gas bubble in her stomach. So, I eased up and let her control the show because she obviously has something to prove.

"Oh, baby, you feel so good. I love how you let me take control! This is just right for me!" Bella professed with her eyes closed. Only, she wasn't talking to me. There is no man on earth, whether big or small, who can't tell if their woman has dipped out.

Three, when paying attention, you discover new habits, like how Bella closed her eyes to imagine riding someone else. She also tried to stick her finger in my mouth, and I fought hard not to bite that muthafucka off! The smell of Bella's essence is different, it doesn't smell bad, but it's undoubtedly different.

"What's wrong, baby? You didn't enjoy me?" she breathlessly pressed.

"No, but you seemed to enjoy bouncing on half my dick, though!" I said to rattle her feathers.

"Here we go with that shit again. I told you I could handle you when you don't get too carried away!"

"Stop fucking lying to me, Bella! You damn near died when

I pushed further inside you. If you hadn't pretended to know how to please me all these years! We wouldn't be going through this bullshit we're going through right now!"

"What is that supposed to mean, Jaylin? You must want to fuck that bitch that was in your office the other day?" She screamed.

I left Bella in the bedroom and hopped in the shower. She tried to shower with me and apologize, but I couldn't hear her words. To me, there was nothing left to be said. I tread to my closet with a wet Bella on my heels! I reached for my track-suit and noticed it was in the wrong spot. Hmm!

"Jaylin, you are not going to ignore me, damn it! I said I was sorry; now, can we move on, please!"

"What are we moving on to, Bella!" I questioned.

"I'll stop!"

"Stop what?" I quizzed, wondering if she would falter into a confession.

"I'll stop working late and pay more attention to you and my son." She said dryly. And that's when I noticed a faint bite make on her neck and the big bouquet of wildflowers.

If I wasn't sure Bella was fucking around on me before, I boldly know now! This particular vase of wildflowers is one of the calling cards of Thee Elite! I just stood there, not knowing whether to choke her out or keep my cool until further notice. Because now her life is out of my hands! All I need now is confirmation on the fool she risked it all for.

"You need to tell the courier to leave a note next time! I was over Terry's the other day, and these flowers were on top of my car! He must have followed me there, leaving the office or something. These are so beautiful, baby, thank you!" She gushed.

"I didn't send you those flowers," I confessed in a daze. "Stop playing, Jaylin. I know you sent these because...." She paused.

"Because you asked your fuck, buddy, and he didn't send them either, huh?"

If Bella was light-skinned, she would be beet red right now! With that, I headed for the door to meet up with my brothers. I have to prepare for my son because he's going to be a motherless child! Not that he isn't already.

Chapter 23 Landin Forest

"**W**hat up, yall? I need to air out some shit real quick! But first, I need a drink!"

"Damn, what's going on? You drinking and shit!" Major remarked.

"Naw, man, I think my wife is setting me up. Sage hired this fine-ass female to be my assistant; I mean, her body is insane. Her curves have curves, and her ass has an ass! Like images of it be sitting inside those chat clouds. And those fuckers be floating through my office every day talking to me!"

These dummies just curled up in the booth laughing their asses off at me! I need some advice, not laughs.

"Nigga you better not get caught up!" Christian spoke."

"I know I'm married, but I'm also human, and my wife knows I'm an ass man. I don't know what Sage was thinking, but she brought an ass of all asses to work directly under me.

And let me not forget how sex drips from her tongue every time she speaks. I'm telling yall she's trying to ascertain my dick!

"Maybe Sage bragged about it or something." Ashton offered.

"You better get control of your dick! It doesn't take but one second for shit to go left!" Jaylin warned.

"I told her she smelled funny before I came here."

"Did she?" Ashton asked.

"No! She smelled good as fuck!"

"Just imagine she has one eye and boogers in her nose. Do whatever you gotta do to keep your dick safe! Ashton advised, rubbing his crotch area.

"Yeah, I bet it's easy for you because my sister loves cutting off body parts." Major laughed.

"Well, if you all knew what I know, there wouldn't be a thought in your mind about cheating. Kiley's been training our wives with her knife collection. I saw a butterfly knife disguised as a fuckin hair clip on Angel's beauty bar. When I turned around to look at her, she winked at me and walked out of the room! I legit got scared!" Christian admitted to being a punk.

Jaylin's appearance is off-setting and has been for months. I know Bella has been on some sneaky shit lately, but this is something else.

"Lay it out, Jaylin!" He hates it when I can see right through him. He let out a sigh and gave us the rundown. And it didn't stop there. Ashton and Christian also had some fucked up news to share!

Bella had me fooled. I knew she was a tad bit standoffish, but grimy was far from my thoughts until now.

"I wonder who sent her the flowers? Either somebody presented it to the elders, and they approved, or one of the elders made direct contact! And we all know what that means." I stated.

"They might not say shit till after it happens. Major muttered.

"Daddy! Can I have a unicorn?" Kelly's innocent face asked. I damn near spit my orange juice out!

"I know they aren't real. I just want a horse, so I can put a unicorn horn on it!" I laughed so hard because Kelly is serious.

"Baby girl, we have several horses on the farm you can choose from.

"I don't want any of those horses. I want my own horse!" Kelly demanded in a demonic voice and with black eyes!

"YOU BETTER MAKE THEM LITTLE BLACK EYES DISAPPEAR BEFORE I GET MY BELT!" I stood up to take my belt off, and she started laughing.

"I was just kidding, daddy, look!" she handed me her phone, and it was a video of kids pranking their parents in that voice! Her ass was about to be walking around here buttless after I got done whooping it off!

After dinner, Kelly took a bath, brushed her teeth, and read along with me as I read her a bedtime story. I didn't want Sage to use that as an excuse for being too tired to prop those legs up tonight.

"Hey, baby, how was work?" She asked sweetly.

"I left early."

"Why is something wrong?" she asked with an unsettling smile.

"Yes, I need some pussy from my wife!" I stood behind her

and kissed her neck. She turned around to give an excuse, so I shushed her with a kiss.

"Kelly's sleep. It's just you and me." I'm so horny I can't see straight! I can smell her essence through her clothes! I haven't tasted her sweet, warm nectar in weeks, and I'm starving!

"Aww! Baby, we can't. I'm.."

"If you say you're on your period, I'm going to assume some shit!"

"I was going to say I'm not feeling well!" she lied.

"Aight!"

"Landin!"

"Naw, you got it!" I walked off from her shady ass! She was just fine when she walked in here! Now I'm supposed to believe she's not feeling well!

Good Morning, Miss Kathy; how are you this morning?" Miss Kathy is not only the secretary; she's the den's mother who keeps everything in line! Including making the interns feel welcome and safe by defusing quarrels and misunderstandings.

"Do you have our New York itinerary for the National Lawyers Convention yet?"

"Yes, I booked your preferred room, and Mrs. Forest booked a room adjoining yours.., never mind. She canceled her reservation. I guess she's not going. I'll double-check later!" I walked to my office confused as hell because why would Sage book a room adjoining mine when she would stay in the same one as me? I hope Sage isn't pulling a Bella! I thought, shaking my head.

Ugh! Why is she in my office leaning over my desk? Fuuuuuuck!

"Oh! Good Morning, Mr. Forest. I had to correct a few shorthand mistakes. Everything is prepped and ready for you to slip and slide right into your day!" This muthafucka, with her word usage, is driving me insane!

"You have a booger in your nose!" I pointed at Emery's nose to get her ass out of my office!

I didn't even look up the watch her ass bounce on the way out! I'm over this shit! I need to figure out what's going on with my wife.

I worked undisturbed until noon, which allowed for a very productive day. Knock knock! I'm going to have to tell her she stinks again.

"Hey, Great-Grandson! I'm here to have lunch with you, so

I hope you don't have any plans." What a fuckin surprise! My Great- Grand Raymond is 96 years old and can still get around like he's 50.

Although I'm grateful for his presence, I can't help but take in his attire. Raymond is sporting a t-shirt that has the letters FYF on the front. And a tracksuit similar to Jaylin's custom-made suits.

"Grand, where did you get that shirt, and do you even know what it means?" I quizzed.

"Yeah, fool, I know what it means; that's why I got them in all colors! His name is Lawrence Wilson, and he said that he could put the label on my suit if I wanted. I thought it was a savvy ass Idea! Fuck Yo Feelins says a whole lot without saying shit. You want a couple t-shirts?" He asked, grabbing his phone.

"Do you have the guy's phone number?"

"Duh, nigga how do you think he's going to put them on my suits. Damn, you act ding dongish as hell sometimes. Jeez!" I couldn't help but laugh at this old man!

"No, thanks. I already have a few of his t-shirts," I confessed.

"Well, then why are you questioning me like that. We

wasted a whole five minutes on something you know about already! Now, where are we going for lunch? I'm hungry after all that talking." Raymond fussed.

Right when I was about to suggest Las Alemedas, Emery walked in.

"LORD, HAVE MERCY ON MY HEART AND YOUR MARRIAGE!" Raymond yelped and looked at me like I was crazy!

Chapter 24: The Birthday Party

Lynn:

Thank you guys so much! You yall did a spectacular job! And in doing so, I put a little something extra in your envelopes! And yes, you all deserve it! The contractors my grandfather hired did everything I asked for and more. The head contractor thought it would be a creative idea to make the warehouse's ceiling look like a sky with clouds made out of cotton candy!

I thought it was a marvelous idea and wished I'd thought of it first! I had them hang up the life-size purple, red, yellow, blue, orange, and green gummies on one side of the room. On the other side, the striped and packaged candies, with the chocolate sprinkle ball sparkling in its own glory.

The floor is painted green with a candy cane road and cupcakes representing climbing levels! Lifesize flowers, cookies, teddy bears, and fruit are half-covered with chocolate. As for the walls, they are made out of actual edible wallpaper! No, I'm not letting any of the kids know! I just thought it would be fun to see who will test it out!

"Hey, ILynn, this is magnificent! I guess we are the first to arrive!" Serta's tight pants-wearing ass gushed. Angel owes me 100 fucking dollars!

Angel:

"**G**OD is GOOD! Mommy, look at all this candy! I want a Minecraft party with candy characters! I'm going to go ask Auntie ILynn right now to hook me up!" CJ excitedly ran off in ILynn's direction.

Aw! Shit, I owe her ass $100! Look at this broad, ignoring the dress code. I really thought Serta was going to heed instruction around kids. Guess I missed the mark on this one.

I'm just going to spray her ass with my chocolate-filled water gun! I came up with that Idea because my mom said that on her last day of high school. Somebody filled their water guns up with bleach and fucked up everybody's clothes. I'm only doing it because I want to win the $1,500 prize!

Yeah, it's cheating, but I'm going to have fun doing it! Besides, I know Landin has a trick up his sleeve! I can tell just by the way he slyly walked in the door. I stepped further into the room and saw how all of the tables were set up. Each Birthday kid had their own set-up with their favorite foods, sweets, and two chocolate fountains sitting on both ends of the table!

I know this heffa is not bold enough to flirt with Major in front of his daughter! Oh! Shit, let me get my cousin before she chokes Serta with a life-size candy cane! I know this is a kids' party and all, but we don't play about our men!

Major:

y wife is the shit! Her vision for design is incredible! I never would've thought of anything like this. Hell, I would've streamed some balloons together in the backyard, barbequed, and called it a day! This looks just like the inside of that game my mother is hooked on.

"Wow! Check out my table, Daddy! Isn't it awesome? We can eat healthy while everyone else gets cavities and blow up like those huge chocolate-covered teddy bears! I wonder what those taste like!" MayLynn licked her lips as she forgot about her healthy kid campaign!

MayLynn and kelly's table favors a featured display in a magazine! There are veggie treats and cheese on one side, fruits, nuts, and vegan cookies on the other side. Instead of a chocolate fountain, they have three salad dressing fountains!

"I think I need to eat at this table with smart nutritional values! I have to keep my figure right and tight! What do you think, Major?" Serta asked, twisting her body from side to side. Out of nowhere, splashes of chocolate appeared on Serta's pants and shirt. When I turned around, Angel was standing there with her homemade water gun!

"Oh, My, God, did you just spray chocolate on me?"

"Yeah, now go get your daughter! She's licking the walls!" Angel cut in before ILynn lost it!

Ashton:

"Tell my wife I'll be there as soon as I'm done installing these cameras," Christian swore out of breath.

"Nigga, you need to get down here ASAP! I just stepped into a game of Candy Crush! Oh! Snap, they got poles with the swarming fish gummies floating in it!

Hold on, I'm about to take a picture and send it to you!" I took a picture and hit send. This nigga is bout to flip out.

"Why is my son licking on the wall?"

"I think it's edible!" I told him, still amazed!

"Go get your nephew off of the wall, please! I'm on my way!" Christian hung up.

What in the world is going on here? Angel is chasing Landin around with a weird-looking water gun! Victorious and Raymond are blocking the little kids from getting any popcorn out of the large Kernal popper! Miss Celia, Rose, and Elenore posed and took selfies in front of the life-size chocolate-covered flowers! And most of the kids are covered in chocolate!

"Daddy! Daddy! Look at the Banana Split I made, mommy! Do you want one!" Ashley smiled. Heck yeah, and bring this little dude some water!" I said, dangling CJ's hyper ass over my shoulder!

"What does the wall taste like?" Kiley asked CJ.

"Like chocolate mint ice cream!"

"And, blue raspberry slushy!" Kyle added with blue lips.

Landin:

The first thing I noticed walking into the party was females in tight clothes. Is this a party for kids, or is this a get chose party? I laughed at this one chick, ripping her pants as she bent down! She knew when she put those pants on, it could go south at any given moment.

I also see a few people with speckles of chocolate on their clothes. That's why I have two changes of clothes stuffed in Kelly's backpack! I'm going to win this money by any means necessary! No, I don't need it! I just want it! Besides that, I'll give it to someone who needs it.

Why the hell is Angel looking at me with suspicious eyes? Oh, hell naw, is that a water gun and is she headed towards me? Shit!

"You better get your ass away from me, Angel!" She squeezed the trigger, and chocolate syrup came out!

She missed me by an inch, so I took off running like a little kid, and this heffa chased after me! I was so dizzy I couldn't see straight. Angel got a little chocolate on my t-shirt, but I got something for her ass. I'm going to change shirts after they cut the cake.

After singing Happy Birthday, I dashed to the restroom. But on the way back, I heard my wife on the phone say,

"Pull out all the stops! I'll be listening!"

The fuck?

Sage:

I'm at the most fantastic party for my daughter, and I can't even enjoy myself. Landin is losing patience with me, and I don't blame him! I just need to know if he really loves me! Emery and Landin leave for New York the day after next, and I'll have my answer.

Mommy! Come sit next to Daddy! I made you both salads!"

Kelly handed Landin and me a bowl of lettuce, cucumbers, tomatoes, grapes, raisins, croutons, with blue cheese salad dressing!

"This is so good, Kelly, thank you! Mommy was so hungry."

"You're something else too, but I'm going to keep that to myself." Landin snidely commented.

This is why I need this to be over so we can go back to normal! I hate refusing my husband. But this test is more critical to my peace of mind.

"Mommy, I think I'm going to go dip this cheese into the chocolate water fountain over there at Ashley and Kyle's table."

I couldn't do anything but laugh! I knew having this candy crush party was going to ruin Kelly's healthy tooth kid campaign! I mean, there is chocolate everywhere! I even was tempted to stuff some of those chocolate-covered marshmallows in my mouth!

Wow! What's up with Jayhlin and Bella? He just walked right past her!

Bella:

"**D**id this nigga just walk past me like I'm not his wife?" i asked myself out loud.

See, that's why I spread them wide for a man who can't get enough of this good thing between my legs! I remember when I was Jaylin's everything. But now I'm shit on the bottom of his shoe! He made it seem like he knew I was cheating, but he was just guessing and hoping I would confess.

I've been cautious, so I just called his bluff! I do, however, wonder about those wildflowers. Who would send me such a beautiful bouquet and not reveal themselves?

"Hey? You not going to speak to your mother?" I asked Junior.

"Hi."

"Wow! Your father is rubbing off on you."

"You weren't here to sing Happy Birthday to me like you promised." Junior spat.

See what I mean; everything is about him now! If I could do it all over, I wouldn't have had him, and Jaylin and I wouldn't be going through this drought.

"It's okay, though, because Dad's assistant and her little sisters sang it to me! So, you can go back to work now."

I wish I could say that hurt my feelings, but I simply didn't have any towards this little attention thief! I, however, am pissed that Jaylin's assistant is trying to steal my spot!

Just when I was about to get in Jaylin's shit, I heard him say, "Let me introduce you to my sister! Kiley, this is..."

"The one!" His sister responded. What the fuck? Am I invisible?

Kiley:

I didn't even let Jaylin tell me her name! Something came over me when I shook her hand!

"She's the one for you; you just don't know it yet!" I whispered in Jaylin's ear.

Bella can walk off of a cliff for all I care, but this one right here. She's God-sent!

"So, how do you like your job so far, future sister-in-law?" Jaylin, and Vina, both choked on their smoothies! I put my arm around Vina and walked off from a confused Jaylin and a pissed-off Bella. Now ask me If I give a fuck about Bella's feelings? You know I don't.

Vina is a much-needed distraction from me wanting to put my foot up Bella's ass! I heard about all the things going on with her. I tried to handle her myself, but higher-ups forbid my request. Bella, better tread fucking lightly, or I'm going to commit treason among Thee Elite!

Now back to the party!

"Are you enjoying yourself, Vina?"

"Yes, I need to hire whoever created this masterpiece of a party!"

"Well, since you're going to be family soon. I'm sure ILynn will give you a discount." I replied while she giggled, probably thinking I'd lost my mind.

Everyone took to Vina like she was family. Look at my brother. They both have apples in their eyes. They stood staring at each other so much as the reason they didn't notice Angel and her chocolate-filled water gun headed their way!

Jaylin:

"AAAA! What kind of water gun is that? That shit hurt like a paintball gun! You've been shooting people with that thing?" I mugged her crazy ass!

"Christian, come get your gun-toting wife!"

First of all, I already knew I wasn't going to win the contest. Every time I wear all white, I get it dirty within 30 minutes of putting it on!

"I can't wait to have kids of my own, so they can experience all this love! You have a glorious family Jaylin." Vina expressed.

"Thank you. I appreciate it. Thank you!" Did I just get tongue-tied? What the hell was that?

"I guess we're both out of the running for the $1,500, uh?" I pointed to the spot of her midsection!

Angel obviously didn't care who you were. If you had on all white, then it was game on!

"Call me crazy, but I'll take chocolate-covered gummy bears

over money any day!" Vina confessed.

"So, you'll be good with me paying you in chocolate?" I acquired, and we both laughed until I felt Bella and Junior standing next to me.

"How the fuck are you over here lolly-gagging with this…."

"Watch it!" Vina warned.

Vina taking up for herself was a must in my eyes, but it was who she held caution to regarding hearing what Bella was about to say.

"Junior, do you wanna go catch some fish out of the poles?" Vina suggested as Bella's face fell.

Christian:

As soon as I walked in. I knew where I was going to post up for the rest of the day! ILynn brought in every damn candy you could think of in Candy Crush. There was a little wall by the smores station, and that's where little CJ and I have been since I got here. Minus signing Happy Birthday to everyone and rescuing people from Angel's cheating ass. Everything is cool!

"Daddy, Mommy should get disqualified from the game! She just shot Nanna Rose and Great Grand Red! Ut oh, she got grandma Celia and grandpa Rumond!" He said in a fit of laughter.

Miss Celia grabbed a paper cup, filled it up with chocolate from the fountain. And she is now chasing Angel around the party!

"Aren't you going to help Mommy?" CJ questioned.

"Heck, naw! She started all this chaos! Don't worry. Your mom is very creative, and she'll find a way out!" I convinced.

Turning to my left, I spotted another wall with Auntie B, crouched down with a bowl of chocolate and cheese! I couldn't do anything but laugh as we had the same idea! Auntie B was so intuned with her guilty pleasure. She didn't see my wife hurdle over the wall landing smack dab on her ass! Angel's clumsiness startled Aunt B, causing her to drop the bowl of chocolate on both of them.

Angel cried in defeat while Mrs. Celia laughed, telling her, "That's what your cheating ass gets!"

Chapter 25: Auntie B

These muthafuckas gone take me out before my time! I couldn't wait to retreat to the hiding spot I found when I walked up in here! I saw Christian and that cute little CJ over in the pod next to me. I'd gathered some goodies of my own and a bowl of chocolate. I hate to share.

That being said, I've also been avoiding my nephews. My sharing issue is why my husband's eye is missing. They're waiting on me to tell the story, and I'm not ready to damn it. That was a really dark place for me! That and the fact that the bitch I caught him with moved away before I could get my hands on her!

My life is in California. I wish I could be a better daughter, sister, sister-in-law, and auntie to my family. But my thirst for payback permits me to move around as much as possible! My enemies are running all over the place, but I always find them with precision.

I've been tracking the homewrecker for months through my husband's e-mail and hers. She's been missing him and has gained momentum and bravery to return to the states. Home-wrecker goes on to boast about my husband's mandingo being the greatest she's ever had.

In keeping with my growing rage, I decided to enlist Major's spectacular hacking skills. I now know what she's been up to for the last six years! My discoveries added fuel to the fire! This bitch was right under my nose! She'd run off to one of my off-the-grid spots in Italy but was recently spotted in Germany. This is why I was already there when the mission was called.

Why haven't I gotten a divorce from my husband's cheating ass? Because I don't believe in divorce. Now the death do us part shit! Right up my alley! Taking his eye was just the begin-ning! I don't think he wants to disappoint me again.

He's been reformed up until a month ago. Not that he said any-thing out of line, it's just that you only have one eye because of the bullshit. You would think a nigga would become fond of the delete button.

I'm not saying I'm innocent in his infidelity. I was busy with my own brand. Yes! I'm a part of Thee Elite, and making jewelry is my cover. However, here and a few other places. I'm known as the Ice Eagle. The reason being, the last thing my victims see is my ice gray eyes!

Hunting for my new jewelry line and not paying enough attention to my husband. Led him right into the arms of a big dick hunter!

Dia was relentless in her pursuit of my husband. He tried to say she drugged him but later told the truth. They met years ago when we were visiting my father, Rumond. I, too, have a house around the lake! Red pays a housekeeper to clean my house once a week.

As duty called, My husband's dick was calling out to Dia. If I'd paid more attention to his body language. I could have caught the shit before it happened. Once our three-month visit was over. We went back to California, where it all went to shit.

Dom started acting more chippy and engaged in what I was doing, where I was going, and when I was coming back! At first, I thought it was cute until common sense hit me in the head. Women's intuition is a muthafucka!

One of my marks walked right into my trap, saving me a whole day of tracking him down. Needless to say, I ended my trip with one thing on my mind! Dom had sent me a text saying he couldn't wait to see me tomorrow night! And with that, I was more excited to surprise him a day early.

When I arrived at my home, I didn't even bother to park in the garage! We have a circular driveway, so I parked there and walked to the front door. Now in all my years of living, I have never been comfortable leaving the front door unlocked!

I walked inside and almost busted my ass, tripping over a red heel! I immediately hauled ass to our bedroom. Only he wasn't in there! So I checked the pool in the backyard, and he wasn't there either. Then I heard moaning and slapping noises towards the garage area!

Dia was in a horizontal split on the front of Dom's car! He pounded into her, smacking her on the ass with no mercy! So, I took out my phone and started recording! Neither of them noticed me until it was too late! I see you have a thing for fake white asses! I spoke to my husband.

I strolled towards them as he was still knee-deep inside Dia's lopsided ass. Dom quickly pulled out, and this bitch thought it would be funny to let out a quick moan as if she missed him being inside of her!

As soon as Dom fixed his lips to say It's not what you think! I plucked out one of his beautiful green eyeballs! Seeing as I wasn't the runaway and cry type of bitch. Dia hauled ass out of my garage butt ass nacked! Leaving behind her purse, phone, and a round trip plane ticket back to Texas.

After reading Dia's full name displayed on her driver's license, I was infuriated to the point of me almost cutting Dom's dick off! This bitch is a member of the White family! Yes, our lifelong enemies. Dia's full name is Nadia White, mother of Amber White.

The mother and daughter duo was supposed to be living their best life far away from the states. But I see old habits die hard! I grabbed a bottle of rubbing alcohol and poured it on Dom's dick. Oh, the screams coming from that man were music to my ears!

The first excuse was rehearsed, the second was a lie, and the third was the truth! I made Dom repeat the third story three times before calling my cousin Melony to treat his injuries. She was in medical school and needed the practice! I often laugh at the look on her face when she laid eyes on Dom's mutilated eye!

Dom said it was harmless flirting at first, and then Nadia became aggressive and daring! He said the first time they had sex was in the bathroom of a restaurant. And the fourth was when I caught them! I could have killed his ass, but his brother Dame is the head of the police department and an ally to the Elite! I couldn't kill him, but I could cut his ass up!

Ping!

Wow! I just thought this bitch up! Dom's email read: *"If you don't contact me! Your wife's family is going to lose everything that rightfully belongs to the White Family! You don't want to be on the losing end of this Dom! Meet me at the Luxury Hotel, room 169. At 7pm Friday evening. PS. Bring that big pogo stick!"*

I forwarded the email to Jaylin, so he'll have time to formulate a plan! He's the strategic one! I, on the other hand, would pluck out her eyes and feed the rest of her body out to the wildflower fields! "

Hey, baby, I just got an email from Nadia." Dom showed me the email, and I couldn't help but smile!

"Yes, Jayln!" I answered.

"We might have to use Uncle Dom as bait. I need both of you to meet me at my office ASAP!"

Ding Dong "BJ? How are you doing, son?" I chirped, while still on the phone with Jaylin.

"Tell BJ to come too! He's just the person I need to talk to!" Jaylin advised.

Chapter 26: English Rivers

My life took a turn for the worst after I lost custody of Zane. I spiraled so out of control, forgetting my motherly duties! I was asked not to return back to the family business until I got my shit together! The love of my life rejects me and treats me as though I don't exist. I know I was a fool over Cain, but deep down, I knew Landin was a better choice for me!

The news of him getting married to Sage sent me into a whirlwind of mass destruction! Then a year later, he and sage had a daughter, and she's the spitting image of them down to her little smart mouth.

Every time I see Kiley, my wrist hurts! And whenever I run into ILynn or Angel, they keep it short!

I've tried countless times to get Landin over here so we could talk! I used Zane as an excuse several times and made attempts to take my life. None of that shit worked, so I went by his job. As you would expect, I was thrown out on my ass! Landin blocked my calls and every social media outlet.

I was even removed from being a Sunday school teacher. Landin would ignore me at church and pretend I had a disease! I purposely spoke to him in front of the Pastor, and he still ignored me. He told the Pastor the devil was in the building and needed some blessed oil to splash on me.

I had to get him back somehow, and that's when I started saying mean things to Kelly. I knew he would come knocking on my door, ready to put his hands on me. I set up cameras in the living room and bedroom. Just in case my plan worked. I'd plan to stick him with a syringe of potent goodies I mixed together!

I was going to make a nasty freaky porno and send it to his precious little wife! I was butt-ass naked waiting by the door when I saw him roar his truck into my driveway! He opened the door, paused and shut it back closed, backed out, and sped off like his truck was on fire!

I was outraged! People at church started whispering and gossiping about how I taunted Sage with old pictures and shit that I would make up to piss her off. Nothing worked, absolutely nothing. I even faked a panic attack in the coffee shop, and Landin just laughed, and walked out of the door!

I tried going out on dates to get back in the swing of things, but they all failed. I compared everyone to Landin, and they never measured up. Venturing on a new dating website, I noticed an old friend who sent a message to my DM! Curious to know what she wanted, I clicked the link and was utterly speechless!

Terry was naked with an invitation between her legs, covering her hot pocket. I had to zoom in to read it! It took me two hours to find everything I needed from the invite! It listed strict rules to follow to be permitted entry. Three hours later, I was sitting in an underground sex layer!

I didn't have anything to lose. I already lost custody of my son, my mother took my physical rehab clinic. And worst of all, Landin won't even let me apologize, let alone have a simple conversation. All I have left is anger towards Sage because if it wasn't for her slithering in! Landin would be mine.

I enjoyed my first night on the Basement Floor of the strip club. The most exciting part of it was who I met. He talked me right out of my trench coat! I didn't care that there was a room full of strangers. Or that this guy was staring at me like his last meal! I was in a trance with his words so I ran my hand over his tattoo, which read. B.J.W.

"Good Evening, my name is revenge! I've been watching you, wanting you, and needing you to see me! I'm on your lips. (He kisses me). Your nipples harden when you think of me. (He

pinched my nipples). I'm tightly tucked angrily in your belly. (he kisses my belly button). I make you so hot, you melt on my tongue (He french kissed my sweet peach). You hold me in your death, gripping thighs. (He caressed my legs with his fingertips) Your feet need direction, so I'll guide you every step to ecstasy! (He placed my feet on his shoulders as he slid revenge in and out of me. For everyone to see!)

I didn't care who was watching! BJ turned me out in that room. He put me in every position you could think of, and I loved it! Though his member wasn't Landin's big pole, it was a nice size! Revenge is mine, and if you don't know by now, **I am the OG!**

I don't know how the opportunity to reign revenge fell into my lap. But I am, however, grateful for it! Being humiliated has taken a toll on my mental.

To formulate our plan, I had to move to Germany a few years back. BJ introduced me to his team leader, and from there, we devised our plan!

We found a private investigator exceptional in his craft! He refused at first, but we found a way to convince him otherwise. His sister Emery has been a fucking diamond in the rough for us. We didn't have to force her hand. Emery came willingly and happily! Her first mission was to finesse Christian and get all the information she could on his business.

Only his lovesick ass didn't take the bait. I wanted Emery to try Major next, but his love for ILynn would have put her in a box. As time went on, I thought changing Emery's appearance would magically work in our favor. Emery has a humungous ass for days, and that's just what Landin loves. Big asses have always been his weakness!

Landin fell in love with my plump fluffy bodacious ass before he knew my name! So, I knew Emery's booty would make him forget his marriage status!

Imagine my surprise to find out about little miss Sage's insecurities. I knew she wasn't ready for my man! He doesn't need a puppy! Landin needs a full-grown bitch!

BJ urged me to become a member of the underground Hats world, and I must say I've fallen in love. Not just with the money, but with the attention and perks! I'm not going to pretend like my feelings weren't hurt when BJ pursued Bella's entitled ass! I guess his plan was to hit his targets from every angle!

I wonder how she would feel knowing Terry has been sleeping with him years before they met! I just might have to be the barrier of bad news because he hasn't taken a bite of my sweet peach in months. Causing me to have withdraws!

The threesomes BJ, Emery, and I had were mindblowing! Bella came along, and Terry, once again, became his favoring flavor.

In that same manner, I started having sessions with Sonny! Another well-known member of Hats. The things he did to my body would make you slap ya, momma! I wonder why he hasn't called me back. He usually answers on the first ring when I do! Ding! Dong! My doorbell jarred me from my thoughts.

What the hell is Jamie doing here?

Chapter 27: Jamie Winters (White)

Years ago, when I told Billion who the key players were for his revenge quest! I wasn't expecting him to be fucking them in open rooms at Hats! Don't get me wrong. It's none of my business who he's doing. It's just dumb as hell to create a flock of females just to turn around and get revenge on him!

I just walked out on my family for good a few hours ago. They tried to give me an ultimatum! Apparently, I've been spotted coming out of Sonny's home on several occasions for the past month. Sonny and I thought up a thrilling idea to say that I needed a place to stay. He told his wife it would only be for three months, and she agreed, and Sonny and I have been humping like rabbits ever since!

Just like always, she kissed her wine bottle until nothing was left! She made it easy for me to slide into their bed! And now it's going to be hard to get me out of it! Hopping up and down on Sonny's joystick is all I could think about! While my grandmother humiliated me in front of our family!

I mean, who are they to tell me who to let loose between my legs! I'm grown. "Either you stay on your meds and let us continue to help you. Or, you walk out of that door for good! I love them, but I love dick more! Due to this, I walked out that door, never to return!

Why can't they just leave my personal life alone! Yes! I was almost killed over doing the same shit, but this is different! I really feel like Sonny loves me! He just doesn't want to leave his wife's money!

To the same degree, I don't want to leave him either. After he divulged his feelings about our relationship. I did some digging in my spare time. In searching, Tammy reversed their prenuptial agreement years ago! If they divorce, Sonny gets 500 million dollars! I'd say he's winning until I saw how much she was worth!

Tammy's net worth is $3.5 Billion! I'd marry her ass if she wanted me to! With the way, things are going thus far. Tammy's going to drink herself to death, and that will warrent Sonny her entire fortune.

"Hey, babe!" I greeted Sonny when I walked into the house.

"Shh! Don't say that shit out loud! You're going to get us busted!" Sonny spat.

"Whatever, she's probably sleeping, Sonny, relax! I went to check on Tammy, and sure enough, she was face down on her side of the bed! Sonny walked up behind me and grabbed my hair violently and pushed me to my knees.

As I milked and twisted his palsating soul! Tammy sat straight up! Sonny pushed me down to the floor, and I scooted under the bed!

"Why are you naked, Sonny? Did I just hear Jamie in here?" She slurred, and that made me so wet!

"You're drunk, Tammy. Go wash your face or something!" Sonny advised.

"NO! SONNY, I heard her in here making slurping sounds." I took the time to search for the wine bottle she supposedly drank from, and it was half full! Shit! Tammy's not in her typical stupor!

"I'm sure you were dreaming! I've been laying here dosing off." He lied.

"You should take a shower! Your thing is hard, and I'm not in the mood for you, Sonny!" she whined.

Wow! I thought! She has a husband with a monster, and she

disregards it and calls it a thing! That's why I'm here to massage it and keep it warm!

That hot feeling came over me, and everyone knows from before what happens!

"What is that sloshing noise, Sonny?"

You need to get in the shower because I don't hear anything." Tammy stalked off to the bathroom! And in one instant, Sonny pulled me by my ankle from underneath the bed!

Sonny faced me towards the door, bent me over, and pommelled onto me rapidly until he released! We heard the shower turn off, and he pushed me out of the room and onto the floor! Then he shut his bedroom door in my face, and I laughed! I was devilishly satisfied!

I heard Tammy say, "I see you pleasured yourself with my lotion while I was in the shower!

Now we can sleep. I just shook my head and continued to the guess shower. On my way there, I noticed Sonny's phone on the counter beeping back to back! My eyes bulged out of my sockets when English's name popped up! I read every single message between them and was furious!

I hopped in and out of the shower, quick as hell! I lotioned up, put my hair in a high ponytail, and threw on my maroon

Adidas tracksuit and tennis shoes! My mother taught me a few fighting techniques after my attack! So I was going to go and show English what I've learned!

English can't have my man! And I'm going to make sure she gets the message through her thick humungous ass! One of the treads read how he would punish her because she came too quickly in one of their sessions. The next one read how her ass still hurts from his bite marks!

That was it for me, and now she is going to pay! I stuffed my whip inside my duffle bag and jogged to the front door!

"Where are you going, Jamie?" Sonny grabbed my ass, and I almost forgot what I was about to do!

"You are on punishment from this dick until further notice!"

I didn't know why I wanted to kick him in the dick, but what he said hurt my feelings.

"So, who are you going to be fucking on in the meantime, uh?" I stared into his eyes, wanting to cry. I didn't care for his dominant character down in the dungeon! Bitches felt like they were entitled when they had sessions with him!

"Who the fuck are you talking to like that, Jamie? He grabbed my neck! But he forgot I love it when he does shit like that!

"Let me go. I'm leaving!" Sonny squeezed harder, and my anger grew more and more towards English! I kept thinking about how he would give her the attention that's meant for me instead!

"Sonny grabbed my neck and muttered,

"You better have your ass back here in two hours! Don't make me come after you!" I ran out of the door and jumped in my car. English stays 30 minutes away from Sunny, and it's going to take me at least 20 minutes to whoop her ass!

Knock! Knock! "Jamie, what are you doing here?" she said with the funkiest expression on her face! I busted right through the door!

"Excuse me! I don't deal with you, on any level bitch! We don't run in the same circles!" she rolled her long-ass neck.

"Oh, no? Who do you think pointed revenge in your direction?" English stepped back as if she was trying to catch a resemblance of my features!

"What are you getting at, Jamie?"

"Anyway, that's not why I'm here. I'm here to tell you to stop having sessions with my man Sonny!" She laughed so hard she fell on her sofa!

I grabbed my whip and started whooping her ass! She's not laughing now.

"YOU! NEED! TO! STAY! AWAY! FROM! SONNY!" The welts on her skin will have her in the house for months!

"Uhh! Stop, you delusional bitch!" Why did she say that? I whopped her head, and she passed out!

"Wake up, cow. I don't have time for this!" I dumped the mop bucket of water I saw in her kitchen on her! She woke up screaming obscenities, and I couldn't help but teeter over! "If you speak one word of this to Sonny! I will show your grandparents a little video I acquired."

I know recording the actions of the patrons in Hats is forbidden, but I needed leverage.

"Where is your Phone?" I asked. She pointed to the coffee table. I went straight to Sonny's name, and his dick size was in parenthesis. I immediately became curious about Landin's.

Ha! Landin's name has my husband and 11inches in parenthesis! Damn, those Forest men are packing something dangerous in their pants! I went back to Sonny's thread and typed in: **I can no longer engage in sessions with you. I am pleased to say I've accepted BJ as my Dominant! No further contact will be made.**

Sonny instantly responded, **"Understood."** I smiled and

showed English the message! Her eyes grew wide! "BJ is my brother! Billion John White. I sent the video of her, Terry, and Billion having a threesome to her phone! Checkmate bitch!

Chapter 28: Jaylin Forest

I bet you all were thinking that their BJ was our BJ! Hell naw! BJ's Government name is Brandon Jacobs. His alias is Barny Jingle Whipsickles! We all fell out when he told us that shit! Who in their right mind would hire someone with that name?

Brandon is our cousin who helped us tow the high school kids to the junkyard for those who may not remember. Cain hired them to shoot Landin and Zane. Lacking common sense, They ignored their surroundings and was nearly sent to their deaths.

Landin had a change of heart and due to the kind gesture. They are all TSU graduates! I guess they took heed to their second chance.

"I set up the conference room for you. There are fruit and veggie trays, Gatorade, and water. I also popped some popcorn for the Great-Grands." Vina assured.

"Thank you, Vina. They'll love.."

"Aww, hell yeah, I'm about to tear this food up! What up, Vina? How are things going over in your new job? Jaylin hasn't tried to kiss on you yet has, he?" Landin shamelessly asked.

"Nigga if you don't stop talking crazy!" Landin laughed, but Vina's face was flushed with embarrassment.

"I'm sorry, Vina, Landin can be a bit.."

"Judicious." She stated. I chuckled at her word choice.

She almost looked as if she wanted me to cross that line, but I don't cheat. That's never been my thing. Until my divorce is final. I'm going to stay on this side of the line as long as possible.

"Aww, shit, is that popcorn? I thought I was going to have to cut out of this meeting early!" Victorious waltzed in here like a cool cat!

"How you already up here, fool? You were supposed to wait for me so I wouldn't get lost!" Great-Grand Raymond fussed.

"You wanted me to wait for you like I was yo woman or something!" Victorious countered. Raymond was about to respond but was distracted by the popcorn!

Raymond grabbed a bowl and sat down, and started smacking on his guilty pleasure! Major snook in without me seeing him!

"What up! You good?" I checked as he was frowning at his phone!

"Yeah, just somebody I'm gonna kill." He responded nonchalantly. I shrugged my shoulders because once he says it, it's a wrap!

Once everyone arrived, I began with a video. It showed some activity of a threesome featuring Terry, the wolf, with his back turned and yours truly, English Rivers. Landin shook his head and chuckled. Sage jumped up and stormed out of the room! And Victorious and Raymond leaned to the side to get a better look at the video!

"Close ya eyes, you old perverts!" Red teased while looking out his peripheral! Grandmother Rose pinched Red, causing him to yelp, and the Great-Grands fell out! While I was reading the room. I noticed Elenore and Victor Sr. weren't sitting together, which is odd because they feel on each other like horny teenagers whenever I see them.

ILynn and Angel were on their phones playing Boogie Babies Bingo with not a care in the world. Brandon is gearing up his video footage, and Auntie B is staring at Landon with her eyebrows raised. My parents are staring at the video waiting on the white wolf to turn his head, and Sade, Jamie's mother, is also viewing the video with curious eyes!

'Uh, Landin, what's wrong with Sage? Aren't you going to go after her?" "I don't know what the fuck is wrong with her! Running out of here like a damn kid! Her ass hired a sex object for her replacement and has the nerve to get mad at a video. Fuck out of here!"

Usually, my mom would have slapped him upside his head, but she could tell like everyone else. Landin is irritated and confused.

"Where did this video come from?" Uncle Dom asked. Jamie's mom Sade got up and walked to the front of the room. "Lately, I've been following Jamie. Sade informed.

"She's been swamped! At first, Jamie was doing well with taking her meds and going to her meetings. During the time between meeting back up with her old music teacher and being dismissed by Major. She threw caution to the wind and joined her brother's team to take us down!"

"She doesn't know anything but speculation, so how is she going to help him? Elenore asked.

"My guess is she pointed Billion in the right direction! I would have come to you sooner, but I had a hard time getting into her phone. Since then, I put the chip Major created on her phone to record her every move!

I found the other journal Billard was hiding! I suppose Jamie didn't believe he had a son, so he gave her the journal as proof. Billard was not only sick but twisted and unaccepting of defeat. If the Judge wasn't being bribed. We could hand the journal over to prove this is all bullshit."

"Major, did you find what he has on the judge?" Victorious asked. Major came up and typed some shit on my computer, and the whole room gasped!

"Judge likes eating chocolate ass! GOODNESS! THAT'S ONE HUGE BOOTY!" Raymond gushed. "Is that a HERSHEY Candybar tattooed on her left cheek?" Victorious made a biting expression.

"Damn! You can't even see his face!" Red expressed. Major hit another button, and this is the one he probably doesn't want to be shown to the public!

"Aww! Hell naw, turn it off! Red shouted.

"Oh! No! You were just in here hooting at the big ass that was displayed on the screen! Now you see him sucking on a d...."

"Okay, Rose!" Red countered and covered his eyes! In this screenshot, you can see a clear view of the Judge's face.

"Damn! The judge has a big...."

"You better not say it, Ella! " Victor Sr. warned.

Do you know who gave Billion the journal Sade? Ella enquired.

"I do." Auntie B admitted. I'm not going to go into full detail, but Billard's book of demands didn't just show up. Nadia was sent special instructions to give him that book from Billard's will. I know this because.."

"I had an affair with her." Uncle Dom confessed.

"The fuck?" Red yelled.

Auntie B shook her head, speaking silently for him to stand down!

"I had a weak period in our marriage."

"Period? So, that means you slept with her more than once?" Elanore questioned.

"Yes, the last time was at our house in California." Auntie B forced out the information. "Thus, when I found out who she was! She'd left her purse with all her personal documentation.

Despite everything, I've been tracking her through her email. The start of all this fuckery. Began with Martha's will, and somehow she found out Nancy claimed her and Amber's inheritance. Therefore she is on the warpath!

As far as her seducing my husband. That remains unknown.

The email she sent Dom was deceiving him to believe she was on the winning side. I need to be granted access to her death! Only me! I have something special in mind!"

"You got it!" I assured. "Brandon, of many hats, your up next!"

Brandon is a tow truck driver, a bail bondsmen, and a private investigator! It's called too much money! And too active to sit down and enjoy it!

"Upon reporting the quote on quote surveillance of you all. I altered a few dates to make it look like a regular routine. I've also been following the women who hired me. She looks very different from the pictures you've shown. Seems she's had plastic surgery and fat from her liposuction put into her butt. Nadia, however, didn't remove the mole she has on the back of her right ear.

This is the address she continues to go to daily. Sadly to say there is no trace of the mystery man ever visiting that address. However, there is a female named Amber, who also comes in and out of that address. The room number at The Luxury Hotel is where she's been the whole time under Karen Kent."

Here is a picture of a man she met at the clubhouse. He never turned around, and when I got a little closer, he vanished.

"This is a photo I found online from a New York Broker convention," Major added.

"That's Billion. He's identical to Billard's build and has the same hair and eye color." Sade concluded.

"Here's what we're going to do! We go on about our day, but be very aware of our surroundings. When the time comes for the sheriff's order to vacate. We'll retreat to the bunker and watch the bullshit unfold from down there! I advised.

After the meeting, I called Ashton and Christian to brief them on the plan. It's unfortunate that their problem is mine as well.

Chapter 29: Billion

WAP! WAP! WAP! WAP! That is the sound Bella was making as she bounced up and down on my Viagra endorsed dick! Between her and Terry, I can go all day sometimes, one after the other. Bella doesn't know I've been fuckin Terry for quite some time now!

Terry was my first taste of chocolate, and I can't get that taste out of my mouth. I get so excited when she's around and frustrated when she has to leave. Bella is a beast sexually; she may even be better than Terry. But Bella is just a pond in this game. The fact that I'm sleeping with a powerful niggas wife is exhilarating!

Terry told me stories about what Bella would do for attention. I played on that shit. And now here she is, risking it all for some dick I let her control. Once I make her see, I'm all she needs. She'll leave Jaylin if he doesn't leave her first! These muthafuckas are rich, and I want it all. I know she'll clean up in the divorce, and I'll take that too!

I was a broker on wall street doing well for myself until I got involved in a pansy scheme that sent me running to the other side of the world. Five years ago, a little birdie, namely my aunt Nadia found me. She sat me down, giving me the whole spill on my family's beef with the five families.

She came up with a way to forge a fake will and a few judges to bribe. I was all ready to walk out of the door. I didn't want to cause anymor problems for myself until the mention of retrieving billions of dollars and land was mentioned. Although my great great grandfather didn't leave his family one red cent. The thought of a fucking black family living high and mighty on land that should be ours. Made me ill as fuck!

In my father's journal, he spoke of all his transgressions. Billard was a sick son of a bitch! He was a sex-crazed freak for black women. The things Billard did to my mom were humiliating! He would make her put on melanin make-up just to satisfy his preference.

I think. No, I know Billard passed down his oversexed gene if that's even a thing. I'm a fucking Dom in an underground sex club. The amount of control I get to have and get off simultaneously is winning in my book! Not to mention the money people pay per show!

The Dominate role became an alter ego. I almost love it

more than I love the money. But that obviously came from my gene pool.

"Baby, am I making you feel good?" Bella whined.

"I forgot she was on my dick. These pills last forever!

"Yes, baby, you feel so good" I faked an orgasm so she could leave. I'm juggling four bitches. Terry is my main, Bella is a pond, Emery is a breadwinner, and English is motivated by revenge. I just may be an addict drinking all this blackberry juice.

"You didn't seem like you were into it this time BJ! Let me find out you fucking on somebody else!" I almost lost control. I will most definitely sock a bitch in the face if they get out of line. Nonetheless, she is a walking money piece to my puzzle.

"Listen, I've been a little distant because you won't open up to me and tell me about your family. I told you everything about me, and I'm sorry, but you feel like a stranger." I pretended to be hurt, hoping it worked.

"Aww, baby, what do you wanna know?" Bingo!

"My family comes from money, and as long as I have been alive. I never had to worry about anything or anyone. My parents worked out of town all the time and were killed in some kind of ambush! No! I don't know who or what.

I was left to take care of my grandparents, which was a pain in the ass! It took away from my vibrant life! The it-girl was no longer! Because she was covered in old folks' smell all fucking day! They died within a year apart from one another.

Events after my grandparent's death took a turn for the worst with my remaining family members! I felt an unjust was done until I recently took it back! Jaylin gave me his undivided attention, and I couldn't get enough of it. I lived a happy married life until my son was born! Jaylin put me on the shelf like an old dusty-ass book with torn discolored pages.

Jaylin owns security firms here, Kansas, California, New York, North Carolina, and England. As of late, I've been thinking about putting my name on his business to make decisions. He'll pay attention to me then instead of that little attention snatcher."

Damn, she's cold! I never pegged her as a shit mother, but when exposed, women like her are full of surprises.

"So, did your parents leave you with any money? I asked. I know the answer to my own question. I just want to see if she'll tell me she's fucking loaded. Even without her husband's money.

They did, and while I have my own money. I still want Jaylin's as well!"

"You won't have to worry about it much longer. Just trust me!" I said, rubbing her back

I need Nadia to assemble a better team. The last one was mutilated! Nadia refuses to admit Jaylin and his family aren't about that life, but somebody got to them!

My family was evil and pissed a lot of people off! I, however, beg to differ on other enemies gouging their eyes out! I think there is only one way to test my theory, and that's to attack them in a public place! And I know the perfect spot!

"Hey, did you say your cousin's birthday party is next Friday at the Layers club?"

Chapter 30: The Test

Sage

"Thank you! Mrs. Forest, enjoy your stay!"

"Thank you, and can you not mention my being here to my husband when he checks in," I gave Allen $300 to keep my secret! Once I made it to my room, I had time to reflect on what possibly could happen tonight.

I couldn't believe how Landin was so intuned to his ex having sex in that video! I mean, he didn't even bat an eyelash. Then he chuckled as if he enjoyed the view of her gigantic ass! I couldn't take it; I had to get out of there. I felt hurt and embarrassed that Landin didn't even run after me! And it's the same reason I'm more eager to run this test!

I used still being angry with him as an excuse not to sleep in the same room! Sometimes anger and resentment cause you to rebel. I thought long and hard about my decision to do this. I had divorce papers drawn just in case he broke our vows. I can't be with a cheater no matter what the circumstances are.

I know I'm not playing fair, and he may be a little upset once this is revealed, but we'll be back to normal if he passes the test.

"Hey! Emery. Now, remember not to take it further than him touching you. You are to hit the wall, letting me know he failed.

Emery

I was so fucking excited I couldn't keep a straight face. Sage is as dumb as a pair of dumbbells. If she thinks I'm not going to let her husband fuck me silly. She's got another thing coming. I'm going to make it really hard for him not to resist me! Landin might skip the touching and dive right into my freshly waxed kitty cat! I could tell Sage was exasperated by my choice of ho gear, but what did she expect?

I informed English of this sweet, sweet day, and she was more excited than me! Sage gave me the perfume Landin loves, and I sprayed that shit all over the room. I can't' wait to see his face when he walks in here! The temptation and tension we've built up being around each other are insane!

I sat on the bench in front of the leather tuft king-sized bed. Just in case things go my way. I want to at least get a taste before I alert Sage. As soon as I heard the door click. I put my hands in my sweet whipped pie. I wanted him to see how creamy it was for him!

Landin is one of the sexiest men I've been around! The

sight of him would make you melt inside! When he stepped into the room, he was looking down at his phone. I could tell the creamy wet, stirring sound coming from between my legs, halted Landin's steps. The moment he chuckled and bit down on his bottom lip! I knew I had him!

Landin sat his briefcase on the coffee table, then took off his suit jacket. He loosened his tie and pulled it over his neck! I don't know why that made me wetter, but it did! I tried hard not to moan at how good I was making myself feel! He's done nothing but enters the room, and I'm on the brink of climatic bliss!

There is a wall with a large size shelf on the side of the bed! I watched Landin perplexed as he stalked over to the wall revealing the safe to unlock it. Oh! Fuck is he putting on a condom? I saw Landin reach into the safe and then his pants. Fuck, his dick is humungous, just like English bragged.

Landin walked back towards the coffee table and picked up his tie! When he reached me, he slipped the loop of his necktie over my head, and I exploded all over my hand! I wasn't prepared for when his lips brushed up against my ear!

Landin

I sat upfront with the pilot of our family jet! I needed to vent and didn't feel like stewing in silence! The pilot is our cousin and Nana Rose's niece! She is also a great listener and gives blunt advice, just like Nana Rose! We weren't kidding when we said our families were well educated and versed in all trades of life! Whatever we need, we can get it from within the Elite.

"I don't know what to say about this one, Landin! It just seems odd she would act like that, considering how you all began! Maybe she feels insecure about something!" Lenise advised.

"Shit, have you seen her? What the hell would she have to be insecure about! That fine muthafucka makes me work out extra hard looking at her ripped body and fluffy plumped ass!"

I'll be damned if I let myself go while walking around with a hotwife. Shit niggas would try snatching her ass every chance they got!" Lenise laughed so hard, causing a little turbulence.

"Yall need counseling, Landin!"

"She needs counseling. I'm copasetic, and I'm the same as I was when we married.

"This shit came out of nowhere, Lenise! It was like a light switched off, and so did the pussy! I mean sex."

"Yeah, after you told me about your new assistant. I thought she had to be insane to put sexy women like that in her place. It's like asking for trouble!"

I thought about Lenise 's last statement. "Naw, Sage wouldn't do no dumb shit like that!" I tried to convince myself. When I reached the front desk, one of the clerks damn near knocked the other guy on the ground to get to the desk first.

"Good Evening, Mr. Forest. I have your key here, and you're all ready to go!"

"Danm, man, you might need to stop drinking those energy drinks. You're hype as fuck!"

"Naw, we just have a competition going on who can check in the most guest. I'm winning as of now!" We both laughed.

I love this Luxurious hotel! The floor I reserved only has two rooms on it! The penthouse and an adjoining room for the kids and cousins that watch them when they come. When the elevator doors opened, a familiar sent blessed my nose! That or

I'm just feening for my wife!

I took out my phone to text her.

Me: Hey! Baby, I made it. Tell Kelly I'll call her in a bit. Love yall!

My Love: I love you too! If everything goes well, I'll be home with a big surprise and dinner tomorrow night!

I was happy as hell! I haven't had Sage's cooking in weeks! Maybe I'll get some pussy after dinner! Shit, I might leave this convention early and make it home before dinner! I was just about to text her back to tell her that her perfume's scent is still lingering from our last visit! But the sound that will make any man weak as fuck stopped me in my tracks!

I can't explain the wave of emotions going through my body! Flashes of thoughts and realizations breached my brain. Emery is sexy as fuck! She has a dark brown lace bra and panty set with a garter belt fastened around her tiny waist! Her inviting wide hips poked out evenly. The six-inch stilettos propped up her legs, giving me the perfect view of her creamy gushy center.

Emery's hair was in a high ponytail and with hooded eyes. The red lipstick enhanced her pouty, luscious lips, and I could smell my wife's perfume in the air! Emery's intentions are clear! After I took my tie off, her sound effects became louder.

There are a total of five lockboxes in this room! I went to my favorite one to shield myself! As I walked over to Emery and stood right in front of her open legs. She came all over her hand after I slipped the necktie over her neck. I watched her busty full breast bounce with excitement as I whispered in her ear,

"What's the plan?"

Emery's breath caught up in her throat, and her body turned into a fucking statue.

"I don't know what you're talking about!" I tightened my tie around her neck!

"Don't lie to me, sexy!" I flirted.

"I'm," I pulled the knot more, and her face started to change to a deep red color!

"Tell me the truth!" What she said next was very tempting!

"Fuck me first, and I'll tell you everything! I unbuckled my pants and reached for my shit! I held it right at the opening of her sweet treat and licked my lips! Emery's eyes grew wide, and from there, I knew I had her attention.

Emery sang quietly with quivering lips, but you would too if you had a big ass Glock pointing at your pussy! Justin, English's brother, runs Jaylin's security firm in New York. Justin makes sure I have the protection ahead of time whenever I'm in town!

My heart was pounding in my chest so hard you would think it was trying to jump out!

"Here is what I want you to do! I want you to get on the bed and do what you were doing when I walked in here!"

Emery climbed on the bed, and I almost said, fuck it! I also noticed something else! I took my phone out and snapped a picture!

"Get it real wet, and when you're about to cum, moan as loud as you can!" I stood there and watched her while she stretched into a horizontal split and got to work! I licked my lips and glared at her intently to give her momentum despite me still holding the gun.

"Aaaaaaaah Uh Uh Uh Uh Uh Oooooooooooooh!"

The way that orgasm ripped through Emery's body. Damn near got her nominated for an Oscar! BOOM!

"YOU CHEATING MUTHAFUCKA! I CAN'T BELIEVE YOU..."

"YOU WHAT! Finish what you were going to say, SAGE!"

"I, I, I thought you were fucking her! She was screaming and yelling like.."

"Like I was blowing her back out?" Sage had a folder in her hand when she busted through the door. "What's that in your hand Sage?" I asked while she stood there, mean-mugging the shit out of Emery!

Sage

I sat in my room, ready to call this shit off! It seemed like all the senses in my brain came back at once! What the fuck am I doing to myself, my marriage, and my family! I was just about to go into Landin's room to get Emery out of there. Landin's text came through, and it was too late! I sat there with my fingers crossed with hope in the pit of my belly!

Five minutes turned into ten minutes and then twenty! "AAAAAaaaaaaa! Uh! Uh! Uh! Uh! Uh! Oooooooooooooh!!! I couldn't believe my ears! This bitch was really fucking my husband! And he was obviously fucking the shit out of her!

I tripped over my own feet, trying to grab the divorce papers! My feeling was indescribable as I kicked that muthafuckin door in, cussing and fussing! Too little, too late to retrace my steps. I was caught off guard as I saw Landin standing there with his gun aimed at Emery!

"What's that in your hand Sage?" Landin asked as he walked up to me.

"It's nothing!" I uttered, wishing the folder would disappear!

Landin snatched the folder out of my hands, and I could have crumbled into small pieces! "It doesn't matter anymore because you didn't do anything with her!" I pleaded, trying to snatch the folder from his grasp! When Landin opened the folder, my heart stopped!

I never saw a more disgusted look in my husband's eyes than now! I not only drew up the divorce papers. I signed them as well.

"Where's a pen?" Landin asked as he read over the document.

"You can't sign it because you didn't do what the paper says."

"So, this was a setup?" Landin asked with fury dripping from his tongue.

"No! It was a test to see if you really loved me. I felt like I was pressuring you into marriage too quickly! I don't know what I was thinking, babe! I felt vulnerable as I watched the vain pulsate on Landin's temple!

"A conversation should've been something to think about! I expected you to cherish our vows to a greater degree. Instead, you invite a stranger into our marriage! WHAT THE FUCK, SAGE! That was some gutter-ass shit! And then you run in here with MUTHAFUCKIN divorce papers. he yelled

"So, you thought I was going to fuck up, uh?"

"No! I had faith you wouldn't," I cried.

"STOP FUCKIN LYING TO ME, SAGE! Landin spat from his mouth! I was scared, shitless! "You signed these muthafuckas with no questions asked. You thought that less of me?" he asked, with pain in his voice.

"No! Landin, I'm so sorry. Can we go talk about it in the other room?" I begged while staring at Emery, who seemed to have a devilish grin on her face!

"Talking went out the FUCKING WINDOW!" He yelled. Landin walked to his briefcase, popped it open, and grabbed a pen!

I was devastated! SoI ran full speed to stop him from signing the papers! He threw the folder at me, and my soul died. Tears poured out of my eyes, and my feet became bricks.

"You can go now." Landin looked towards the open door I came out of.

"I'm not going anywhere! We need to talk, Landin!"

"Naw, I'm done talking! I signed your divorce papers. Now get the fuck out of my room, Sage!"

"Come on, Emery" I waited for her to get up, but she didn't move!

"Emery's not going anywhere," Landin said while unbuttoning his shirt.

"The hell she isn't! Get your ass up out of my husband's room!" I screamed.

"Naw, she's about to get your soon-to-be ex-husbands dick! That's why she's here right?"

"Landin! I swear if you touch her, I'm going to...."

"TO WHAT, SAGE? You already signed divorce papers. So we're basically free to do whatever, right? You sent her here to fuck me! So you might wanna get another room. I'm about to make her pussy talk to me because that wet and gushy juice box has been purring loudly" Landin carelessly admitted.

Emery had the nerve to squeal! And I went ballistic! Barricades of a hundred men couldn't stop me!

Landin ran to me and picked me up! When I glanced over at Emery, she was holding her mouth and eye! I thought Landin changed his mind and that we were going to my room to talk. But he dropped me on the bed and tried to leave! I lost it once again by slapping him in the face!

"FUCK!" Landin roared!

"Don't ever in your fucked up life put your hands on me again! You did this to us! Now, if you'll excuse me, I have some pussy in my room! Thanks to you!"

"FUCK YOU, LANDIN!" I screamed.

"You didn't want to! Remember? And with that, he left!

Landin had music playing, and moments later, I heard slapping noises and moaning! I screamed and started beating on the walls until I made myself sick! I ran to the bathroom, puking my guts out, and collapsed to the floor! Then suddenly I could hear Miss Alice in my ear!

"Sometimes actions you cause can never be fixed! Love has already been proven! Take caution, baby girl."

"What have I done?" I screamed

I wasn't expecting the midnight blue irises staring back at me! Mrs, Forest was always lovely to me and treated me as if I were her own. But this look she gave me was of pity and concern.

"Get up, baby girl! Let's get you in the shower. You have puke all over you!"

"Mama Celia, I messed up big time!" I started to remember what happened.

"Listen, Sage, you need to get cleaned up, and I'll be as honest as I can with you," she said sweetly.

That didn't sound good at all. I don't think I'll be able to fathom any more heartbreak.

Emery

I can't believe this shit! A bitch is going to be rolling in the money. I killed two birds with one stone! English has been texting me nonstop! "Stop fucking texting me! You're going to get us caught! Besides, he's about to fuck me silly!

I called English and muted the phone! Overhearing her conversation with BJ the other day made my blood boil! They're going to kill me upon my arrival! BJ feels that I know too much! English transferred $100,000 in my account, and I moved it to a new one! She knows my password and planed to refund herself once they got rid of me!

The whole time Landin and Sage argued, I pleasured myself while face-timing English! The fact that I earned my money destroying their marriage, is a feeling of triumph! I felt like I was watching a theatrical play.

After Sage hit me! I became agitated but quickly recovered

at his tone! When he picked her up and tossed her in her room. I exploded with relief!

"Get up on all fours and show me what that ass can do!" English hung up, not wanting to hear us any longer.

"Put some music on, please!" I shook my right ass cheek and then my left! Landin went towards the wall. I know for sure to get a condom! He came back to the bed with an ice bucket and a bottle of whiskey!

I took the bottle of liquor out of his hand and poured it all over my ass, and then I drank some! Landon took the bottle and poured him a glass as well! He then stood right behind me, enjoying the view of my bouncing ass!

SMACK! SMACK! SMACK! Landin's masculine, large hands slapping my ass cheeks sent shockwaves up my spine! The next set of smacks made me giddy! The 9th and 10th had me dizzy! What I felt next introduced me to the stars, moon, and galaxy up above.

Landin

It felt like the world was a ball lodged inside my esophagus! Sage just broke my fucking heart in two. Emery's WAP sounds were driving me insane! I'm glad she asked me to turn on some music! Because Emery was wearing me down, considering what just went down with my wife and me.

Fuck it! I walked to the smaller safe and took out what I needed. Emery poured half the bottle on her ass! I smacked that muthafucka and said a prayer! I slapped her ass harder and harder to distract her from what I was about to do!

The last slap made her moan louder than before, and I could hear Sage going nuts in the other room! If it wasn't for her, my dick wouldn't be brick hard for another woman! As she moaned, I thumped my syringe and plunged it into the Hershey candy bar tattoo on her left ass cheek. She was out like a light within seconds.

See, when I was in Sage's room, I could hear Emery briefly on her phone! As I walked back into my room, I could see English's face before putting the phone to her side. It amazed me how English pretended to be a woman scorned. When she's the one who kicked my ass to the curb!

I sat in the lounge chair across from the bed for what seemed like hours. I don't like repeating myself. So, I face-timed everyone and told them what happened!

I feel so fucking numb right now! The love of my life is in the other room, not knowing how bad she fucked up! I'll never be able to trust her ass again! As time ran through the universe. I fell asleep.

"Hey, son, I ordered you some breakfast!" My mother gently said.

"Mom, I don't want anything to eat!"

I looked over towards the bed, and Emery was still passed out.

"Don't worry about her son. Your Aunt B is coming for her! I'm going to go check on your wife, okay?" she assured.

"Mom!" I tried to stop her.

"I don't wanna hear it, Landin! I know your hurt right now, but we need to understand the motive. This shit doesn't make any sense!"

I just shook my head and closed my eyes! I thought about how Kelly was going to react to me not being in the house with them!

"FUCK!" I growled

"Come on, son, let's get you out of this hotel room! My father voiced, and I just got up and grabbed my things!

Chapter 31: Major Forest

I n the meeting, I received an alert on my phone showing that Tyra had arrived at the warehouse where we used to store our weapons. Tyra's parents are gun manufactures. The best in the game, if you ask me! I ordered six custom-made 50 Magnum Desert Eagles. All chocolate brown trimmed in rose gold.

The Badducks distribute to many private contractors worldwide, and thus far, the alliance has been great. However, the problem I'm having is watching Tyra remove all of the clips and replace them with what I assume are blanks!

Although the Badducks have been good to us. By providing service at the drop of a dime. It will be unfortunate their daughter will no longer be with us. Once you show me your true colors. That's it!

Last week Red asked me to sort out his order of 357 magnums! He said he had already informed Tyra I would be retrieving them. When I entered the building. Tyra was standing naked in front of the display table. Her fire-engine red waves fell below her waist! Looking like a fucking mermaid under the sea!

She had two gun holsters sitting on the sides of her milky breast! And the other was a drop-leg holster resting in between her thighs. I swiftly unsnapped the holsters on the side of her breast, examed them, and put them to the side! I snatched the gun from its holster resting between her legs, and she moaned while licking her lips.

Tyra then unbuckled the holsters allowing them to hit the ground. Giving me a better view her bare breast and protruding gumball-sized nipples.

"Do you like what you see, Major" Tyra quizzed, jumping up to sit on the table .

" I do, and Red will be pleased!"

"Excuse me? I'm talking about my body! I examined the last gun and put it in Red's lockbox. When I turned to walk out the door. Tyra went in!

"You have got to be the craziest nigga to walk out on a bitch like me!" She spread her legs further. "Just come and get it! It's that simple!" She boasted.

"That's your problem! A nigga like me doesn't fuck with simps!" I left her there, cursing at my back! I have to admit what she did was a bold and daring move! But she's gonna die next time.

However, judging by my rejection to fuck is the motivation behind this foolery I viewed on the video. I got something for that ass, though! I went to the warehouse to check and see what she'd actually done! And I was right! I changed them back and packed them up. The twins are having a birthday bash at their club, and I need to hide the guns there.

Christian thought it would be a good idea to have secret components around the club! His concept couldn't be more genius.

I could smell smoke when I got out of my car! But when I walked into the house, the smell had gotten stronger! I rounded the corner, and ILynn was on her tablet playing BOO-JEE BABIES BINGO! The fuck!

"Uh! ILynn, you don't smell the chicken burning?"

"WHAT! OH MY GOD! MAJOR! This chicken is not burnt!" She turned with her lip up!

"ARE YOU CRAZY? THIS CHICKEN IS BLACK AS FUCK!" I heard somebody calling out a name and then a number!

"YES! I WON!" ILynn was jumping up and down like the kitchen doesn't have a fog advisory!

I picked her tablet up to see if I could get the operator's name! Tamika Anderson! Gotcha. I politely DM'd her and told her to kick ILynn Forest out of this group because her ass almost burned down the muthafuckin house! PS. Please don't re-invite her!

"Hey! Daddy's baby!" I spoke through my phone! Auntie B once again swooped up the kids for a couple days!

"What are you and mommy doing?"

"Starving!" I replied! MayLynn started cracking up. "What is she saying a long prayer like always?" It was my turn to laugh!

"No, she bur.." ILynn snatched the phone! And I laughed harder.

After grabbing some dinner from Lemons Chicken, I saw that I was getting a face time call! "What's up, Landin?"

"Just listen. I need you all to just listen!"

I could hear and feel the hurt in his voice. And I was getting pissed by the minute!..... What the fuck is going on with my In-Laws?

Chapter 32: Billion's Public Display

Billion

"What the fuck do you mean the money isn't in the account English? You better find all that money, or else all this shit we have planned is coming out of your pockets!"

Emery racked up over $800,000 stripping, doing public and private shows at Hats, and doing side jobs!

Being that I'm going to kill her! She's not going to need any of that money! I had to step outside to get in English ass. Because she is the one who came up with all of this bullshit! The dough in Emery's account is going to fund this epic public display showdown!

A woman scorned will always run their mouths about being rejected. And that's how I found out who their gun supplier was! Not about that life, my ass! Tyra was all too fervent to do what I asked! She didn't even consider the consequences of being found out! Tyra and her family could be killed for her betrayal. I can't wait to see their faces when they pump blanks out of their guns!

Bella hit the roof when I told her I was coming to the party! I told her it would be fun and audacious to be in the same room as her husband! She adamantly tore that idea down! I hope when she sees me tonight, she'll come to me. If not, it will be the last time I see her alive. Bullets don't have feelings.

"Where is she?" I asked, heading into my Great grand Martha's abandoned home.

"She should be at her apartment by now. She's not even answering her phone, Billion. Maybe she caught on to what you were planning and ran!" English spat.

"For your sake, you better hope she's still with Landon and lost track of time.

The team Nadia gathered seems to be perfect! They'll blend in perfectly!

"Where are you? You need to get over here so we can go over the plan again! I yelled in Naida's ear!"

"I have my own agenda tonight, Billion! Have at it! After you wreak havoc on those assholes, come to the hotel room! If they're all dead, we won't have to use the judge and this forged will to take over!" Nadia chirped.

The women in this family are so fucking dumb over the black dick! She's lost all train of thought over it!

"Did you at least get the guns?" I asked.

"What? Billion, must I do everything? You need to supply the weapons! There is no way they would have been able to walk through customs with guns, genius!"

"This is bullshit! I don't need your ass for anything else!" I yelled!"

"Your father's instructions are for YOU to take back what belongs to us! Not ME! So, get your boxers out of your ass and go do it!" Nadia hung up in my face.

I called Tyra. Maybe she can help me out with some firepower!

"Alright, guys, this club has many different floors. However, the main party is on the top floor! The club is also connected to a parking garage, so it won't be hard to flee! Remember, shoot at my command only!

I hopped in my car to head back home. I need to loosen the fuck up, and I know just the two who can release my tension.

"Hey, get your ass over to my apartment in an hour!" I demanded in English's ear.

"Hey, baby, come give me a couple scoops of that chocolate fudge!" Terry never disappoints. She'll be here anxious to jump on my face!

English

I'm sick of this muthafucka talking to me crazy! I want these fuckers gone just as bad as he does! I can't even hold my head up high because of them! First, this bitch Emery isn't answering her cell, I can't find the money in her account, and now I have to dip into my stash to pay these so-called hitters his Aunt hired.

If I knew how to shoot a gun, I would kill them myself! I'd just finished putting on a ton of make-up! Jamie did a number on my body, and I can't wait to pay her ass back! If I can't fuck Sonny! I know who I can nudge in my spot! Jamie would be shitting bricks if she knew who I'd befriended over the years!

I walked into Billion's apartment, expecting him to be alone. But Terry's chocolate ass was riding his tongue like a fucking motorbike! He lifted her up long enough to tell me to sit on his thick sausage. I don't know what kind of energy Billion has, but he stays hard for a long time! Terry and I have come at least three times already! He picked Terry up and slammed into her repeatedly until he maxed out all of his soldiers!

"Are you going to the party?" Terry asked me.

"No, she'll fuck this whole thing up by showing her face this soon! Nobody knows we have a connection, and I want to keep it that way!" Billion finalized.

"Whatever! If I want to go, I will! Who the fuck do you think you are to tell me what to do!

SLAP! Fuck! I didn't see that coming at all! "Did you just hit me?"

I ran to the vast vase sitting on the dining room table, and threw it to the ground shattering it into a thousand pieces.

I had tears in my eyes as I bolted to the door, but he got to it first!

"Baby! I'm sorry!" He tried to kiss me, but I mushed him.

Billion picked me up and put my legs over his shoulders. When he flicked his tongue on my button, I lost it! Terry kissed him down below, and all was well again.

"Your, gonna stay home, right?" Billion asked between intense licks.

"Yes, Sir!" Fuck! His tongue is fantastic!

Terry

"I don't think I should go with you tonight!" I whispered to Billion.

"And why the fuck not?" He angrily responded.

"Because I don't want Bella to see us together in that way! She already suspects something.

"Listen, after this is all over, and I have the land and money. Bella will be irrelevant! It's going to be you and I riding off into the sunset!" Billion confessed.

This is what I was afraid of! I don't want to be with Billion! I'm only here for the money and the excellent tongue in his mouth! I know I should have disappeared when I noticed him falling in love with me! Billion introduced me to a whole new world of money! With all the open room shows Billion and I had. Struggling will be a distant memory due to all the Dom's with long money knocking down my door.

"Bella has a whole husband she needs to worry about! Besides, you can tell her you were just showing me around if she asks."

"I still don't think it's a good idea! What if the twins put two and two together?" I pleaded.

"They won't. They don't even know what I look like or that I exist!"

There was no use in continuing my argument with him. I showered, moisturized, and put on my skin-tight navy halter top dress that shows off my thighs! Billion looked so handsome in his navy Giorgenti New York suit!

Billion

The party was in full swing with a spectacular view and great music! I don't think I've ever been this close to this many fine-ass chocolate women in my life! I had to give my man a lashing because he was threatening to pop the button of these tight-ass pants! Damn!

There's caramel, peanut butter, toffee, and coffee in this bitch! Fuck I forgot about the coms I gave the six men I have circulating around the party. Hell, they're probably thinking the same thing.

"Uhm! Billion! I think we have on the wrong shade of blue! Everyone seems to be wearing midnight blue and not navy blue! I looked around and seen a slight difference, but who cares. You really can't tell in the dark areas of the club! I hit up Tyra, and she was able to supply my men with matte black, top-of-the-line desert eagles!

After lusting over the assorted chocolates in the room, I spotted my targets! These muthafuckers are living the life! They were all dressed in Armani gear!

"Hey, do you guys want a drink?" A sexy milk chocolate waiter asked!

"Hell... I mean, yes, I'll take a bourbon neat!"

"Stop starring at her ass, or I'm going to leave!" Terry forced out of her closed teeth.

I heard Terry say shit, and when I looked in the direction of her tone, I noticed a pissed-off, Bella! Her dumb ass is about to give herself away! I couldn't help but smile at my handy work!

I'm going to give this party another thirty minutes before I start ripping through souls! But first, I need Bella to get out of harm's way! My soldiers all have pictures of their targets, so my job here will be done soon! After about three drinks, I started to feel like all eyes were on me!

I looked up at the balcony and got mad all over again! I spotted my men and told them to get into position!

"FIRE!" The gunshots rang out so fucking loud I could feel my ears pop! As I looked around, I noticed my men falling to the ground and my targets still standing. One last single shot rang out, dropping the extra guy I had on Jaylin!

A strange wind coursed through the air as they all stared down at me! I grabbed Terry by the arm and hauled ass out of there! That shit made me feel like I was in the twilight zone! We sped off and drove to the Hotel!

"Did you tip them off, Terry!" I shook her violently!

"Oh! My! God! How could you ask me that! I would never betray you!" She cried!

"Who informed you of the colors to wear to the party?" I'm curious as hell because, if I'm not mistaken. We were clearly identified by our shade of blue like you said! I spat

"Who are these niggers?"

SLAP! She slapped the hell out of me!

"Fuck! I'm sorry, Terry!"

"Get the fuck away from me! I'm done!" And with that, she jumped out of the car!

I practically ran to my Aunt's hotel room only to be met with a note and a bouquet of wildflowers.

Roses are red, violets are blue! Which wildflower will become of you?

Chapter 33: The Elite's public display

Earlier in the evening!

∞∞∞

Auntie B

"**N**ow remember, Aunti B, you have to let Uncle Dom go inside the room first." Jaylin instructed.

"Why?"

"So, he can assess the situation." Jaylin convinced,

"Okay, okay! Now get out of my ear so I can concentrate!" I yelled in my ear coms. They're so bossy! Jeez!

"I can still hear you, Auntie B!" Ugh! Dom, hurry up so we can go get ready for the party!

He knocked on Nadia's door, and the bitch called for him to just open it!

In true ho fashion, this old skank was in a sex swing hanging from the ceiling. Nadia's legs were spread wide into the splits showing her reconstructed vagina! On the table next to her were six different assorted edible oils! "I'm ready for you to ...."

Nadia's voice was caught in her throat when she saw me

standing behind Dom!

"Oh! No, don't be shy now! What were you going to say to my husband?"

"We don't know because your ass went inside the room too early!"

"Jaylin, you said that out loud!"

"Oh, my bad!" I just chuckled at my great-nephew!

"Why is she here, Dom? I thought you wanted to try out my sweet new flower!" she purred.

I walked up to Nadia and sliced open one of her fake ass butt cheeks! The gook that fell out almost made me lose my lunch! Nadia passing out from the pain I inflicted. Gave me time to leave the items I was instructed to place on the counter. The cleanup crew grabbed our cargo and headed to the farm. Meanwhile, Dom and I got ready for the party!

Christian

I sat in my office in total disbelief at what Major discovered. No matter how grateful I am for his findings. I'm pissed that the shit was planned to unfold on my fuckin Birthday. Knock Knock.

"Come in!"

"Hey! Bossman just wanted to say Happy Birthday to ya!" She handed me a navy blue pen!

"Thanks! This is my favorite color! As a matter of fact, that's what I told everybody to wear tonight! No navy blue, no admittance." I chuckled, hoping she'd take the bait.

"Okay, well, enjoy your day!" She pranced. "I will, and Terry. You can go ahead and take off! Your assistant will take over."

"Thank you, Christian!"

Terry doesn't know it yet. But today was her last day as our branch manager! After I sent an email to Major about the color change for our party. I retreated deep into my thoughts.

A couple hours later, Ashton came into my office with a **Cali**

Love Pie!

"Now you know this couldn't possibly taste better than Angel's famous cheesecake!!!" I took one bite and put my head down.

"My wife is a FUCKIN LIER!"

"What are you talking about!" Ashton asked. "Taste this pie!"

"WOOOOOW!"

Major

S hit! I just received an email from Christian telling me to wear midnight blue instead of navy. After he explained, I thought it was a great idea! It's a way to identify the enemies. Now I just have to ease the news to ILynn! She and Angel already bought their dresses! So this shit is going to go one of two ways.

"Hey, love!" She was prancing in the mirror, modeling her dress! Fuck, it looks so good on her! "Baby."

"Unt ah, Major, I know that face all too well! What are you about to say!" She put her hands on her hips!

"Give me a chance to say it, damn! We have to change our colors for the party."

"To what? Do you see me in this dress?" ILynn turned around, slowly teasing me!

I just bit my lip and shook my head. "Yes, baby, but if I recall, you have an even sexier midnight blue dress in the closet you haven't worn yet."

"So, the color changed to midnight blue?"

"Christian told Terry the color for admittance to the party is navy blue!"

"Assuming she's going to relay the message to the guy we've all been looking for. It could be a checkmate type of night!"

"Okay, baby. Now I have to call Angel and Sage. It took Angel and me forever to convince Sage to come!"

"How did that go?"

"I don't want to talk about it! I felt so bad for her when Kiley ripped her a new one! Shit, we were completely speechless after she finished telling us why she did it! Her Aunt Cree had a fucked up way of thinking."

"I don't even want to know!"

I called my parents to tell them about the color change. I trust she'll relay the message to Landin, who's been staying there ever since the bullshit went down with him a Sage. There was a ping on my computer, alerting me of movement at another warehouse Tyra was using!

I didn't trust her after what she'd did, so I had her followed. A shipment of guns arrived in the wee hours of the morning! Me being curious. I went in and inspected 7 Desert Eagles! I politely switched out the real bullets for blanks. Just as she'd done with my shipment.

I zoomed in and turned the volume up!

"You're in luck, Billion! I just got a shipment in this morning! I'm going to grab them and head your way! Major will be sorry he turned me down!" Tyra roared!

"Naw, you're going to be sorry! I said to myself.

"That bitch is going to get cut wide open!" A furious ILynn yelped!"

"Calm down! I'm going to send this video to Jaylin. I got something for that attitude, though!" I picked ILynn up, draped her legs over my shoulders, and moved the thin lace to the side!

"We might be a little late!" As I french kissed my favorite lips!

Jaylin

Man! My Sister-in-Law got it going on with her vision! Who would have thought a few decorations would liven up the place! Silver reflective table clothes were draping the tables. A tall, dark blue vase held a single dark blue rose with silver glitter sprinkled on top!

While I'm happy, everyone got the memo about the color change. I'm pissed that Bella's dumb ass didn't even have on the navy blue as requested. This dingbat has on a red dress with a split up to her waist.

If I hadn't caught on to her bullshit! I would have thought she was the sexiest woman in the room! Now she's nothing to me! The envelope I dropped in my office a while back was divorce papers. I knew if I put the net worth of my company, she would sign without reading! I paid $100.000 for a speedy divorce and received the finalized documents this morning!

Bella's security detail informed me of her location this morning! I'm not going to lie. It stung like hell looking at the footage they retrieved from Billion's open laptop! Watching Bella have sex with another man solidified my actions, and now Bella's belongings are in the process of being moved!

Tupac's Ambitionz az ridah! Came on, and everyone started dancing! I was in a zone when I saw dumb and dumber walk through the door! Remembering they were the guests of honor! I had to stop myself from breaking Billion's long chin.

Billion's crew had sporadically made their appearances two at a time! We offered them several flags to dismiss themselves from this fuckery! One, they weren't asked their names. Two, they weren't searched for any weapons, and three, they are the only ones dressed in a lighter shade of blue.

I stood two feet behind Billion and Terry unnoticed! I watched Bella standing on the balcony as she spotted her lover and best friend standing relatively close! That's when she noticed my glare! I couldn't help but laugh at her stupid ass! I turned to go find my brothers and bumped into Vina!

Vina is a natural beauty with a bright spirit! I did an extensive background check on her. I could see myself with her, but I needed to give it some time. "I need you to come upstairs with me right now!" I whispered in her ear! I felt her shiver. But I was only trying to get her out of harm's way.

Major intercepted Billion's coms and gave everyone a signal on when he authorized his men to shoot! Once we figured out who the targets were. All six of Billion's men stood in front of their targets! Me, Major, Landin, Christian, and Ashton.

These muthafuckas would have killed us dead in front of our family and friends. That is if we were some regular niggas! This is Thee Elite, damn it! BOW BOW BLOC BLOC BLOC BLOC BLOC BOW BOW!!!!!................. You see, all the patrons in attendance at this party are strictly Elite members! Our friends are our family! The fuck you thought!

My cousin Knightly is the coldest of all and the best sharpshooter in all thee Elite! She is my dad's deceased twin brother's daughter and the same age as Major. Crouching down on the balcony stairs. Knightly took out the extra man aiming for my head! And just like that, she was gone!

After decorating Billion's flunkies with holes, the clean-up crew came in and did their thing! ILynn, Angel, Vina, and Sage were pushed into the office. Hell, no, Kiley wasn't in there with them. She was standing right next to me, busting her guns! Yes, she has guns!

The best part was when we all looked down at Billion's pale

face! He grabbed Terry's arm so hard he could have pulled it off.

"What the fuck, Jaylin! You didn't even look to see if I was okay!" Bella screamed! Auntie B started to head in her direction until I stopped her.

"You are no longer my concern!"

Your only option just ran out of here! If you hurry, you can probably catch him.

"What are you talking about, Jaylin? There you go with your paranoid assumptions!"

"Oh, I forgot to tell you, Kendra and Renea came by the house this morning!

They thought you were sick since they haven't seen you in months." Bella's face dropped as I walked away.

Chapter 34: Landin & Sage Forest

I don't want to fucking be here! I thought out loud as I headed for the door. Just as I was about to leave. Sage approached me, smelling like heaven.

"Landin, please talk to me! I miss you so much!"

I mimicked what she just said. "You had my attention day and fucking night but decided to play games. I don't understand what you could possibly have to say to me right now!"

"Please let me explain why I did it!" She pleaded with tears in her eyes! YOU better keep those muthafuckin tears in your tear ducks Sage! You weren't crying when you hired a whole sneaky conniving bitch to set me up! Did you even do a background check on her?

"Just a basic one. Emery's resume spoke for itself!" She tried to save face.

"Sage, you sound real fucking stupid right now! You all but hired her to be my assistant. You hired her to seduce me! Did you know she doesn't even drink coffee? She hates it! In fact, she hates the smell of it! I overheard her in the break room talking about it!

So what you need to process in your mind is why was she in the coffee shop if she isn't fond of it?"

Sage

Landin tried to walk away from me, but I put my hand on his chest! He sucked in a long breath as I searched for his heartbeat! His stone expression made me cringe!

"You can't feel that muthafucka can you!" I shook my head. No!

"That's because you broke it!" Landin flicked my hands away and walked off!

Kiley had her hands up, asking me if it went well! I gave her the thumbs down, and her shoulders shrank! Kiley was pissed at me at first but has been super supportive. I was honestly shocked! I didn't think any of them would talk to me ever again!

ILynn came and grabbed my hand and led me to the dance floor! They played the 90s and early 2000s songs. "Okay," Nivea (feat. Lil John & YoungBloodZ) came on, and all the ladies were on the dance floor! After thirty minutes of playing some of Beyonce's hits! It was the guy's turn! Hell, we grooved to their music choice as well! DJ quick, Snoop Dog, and Dr. Dre's Compton album!

Landin

S hit, I was so glad Ashton told the DJ to change the music! I tried to leave again, and Great-Grand blocked the fuckin door! I'm still trying to figure out how his old ass is still up in here!

"Does Jaylin know you been sneaking into his house through his linen closet to steal his tracksuits?" I laughed so hard at Raymond's shocked face!

"Does Sage know you been sneaking in yall house watching her cry herself to sleep every night? It was his turn to laugh! How does his old ass know that?

"Yeah, just like your ass was following me. I followed you back! I may be old, but I'm still a knowledgeable muthafucka!

"Did yall know the coms are still live!" Jaylin spoke in our ear pieces.

"Ut, Oh!"

I turned around, and Great-Grand was gone!

"Come on up here and holla at me, bro!" Jaylin instructed. I just want to go lay down. Seeing Sage looking so good irritated me! The divorce papers did it for me, though!

Sage drawing up those papers enlightened me of how much she doubted anything I ever said to her! It's just like saying I love you, BUT. I sat up and chopped it up with Christian, Ashton, and my brothers like we didn't just kill some muthafuckas!

I have to admit I was having a good time until some old ass song started playing! "Love Come Down" by Evelyn Champagne King. We looked over at the DJ booth, and Auntie B was standing there with the DJ's headphones on!

"Will somebody yank Auntie B's ass out of the DJ booth! Please! Wait, is she about to play some Luther! Awww! Shit!"

Chapter 35: Bella Banks

"**B**itch, what the fuck just happened back there! What the hell is going on with you and Billion?" I screamed in Terry's ear!

"One, you need to stop fucking yelling at me! Two, how the fuck are you questioning me when you're married to sexy ass, Jaylin? I just accompanied Billion to the party! So, you should thank me bitch!" she fussed.

You were about to blow your cover judging by the way, you're eyes burned through the sight of us!" Terry said, out of breath.

"Why are you out of breath, Terry?"

"I'm leaving this town for good! And you should too!

When I got to my house, my things from work were sitting on my front porch with an envelope I thought was my last paycheck!"

"What was it?" I quizzed. "It was a letter demanding I tell them the truth about the blackout! I'm telling you, Bella, they know you had me take that money!" Terry wined.

"You sound like you're going to snitch, Terry! Do you know what I have on you! I can send you away for life!" I fret.

"Oh, you mean how you used me to make it look like I killed your grandparents? News flash bitch! They know it wasn't me!" Terry hung up in my face, and that's when gas released from my body without permission!

I tried to call Terry back, but she'd blocked me! I drove up to Billion's apartment and parked right next to his car. As I walked up the stairs, I was strickenly dumbfounded. The luggage I had custom-made a few years ago was sitting in front of his door! What the fuck? The door was open as the rest of my things came into view!

"I guess the cat is out of the bag now, uh?" I turned to see Billion sitting on the kitchen counter with a half bottle of Burbon.

"What are you talking about, BJ? Why did you come tonight? "You see all of your shit sitting in my apartment, and your only concern is why I went to a party.

Wake up, chocolate drop! Your husband knows about us and apparently has for a while! Oh, and this is for you!" Billion handed me a folder. "It seems you are a divorced woman now!"

CHARLENE BLUE

I looked through the contents and could have died right on the spot.

"Please tell me you didn't sign and send off these papers without reading them first!" Billion huffed.

I just put my head down!

"That slick SON OF A BITCH! He tricked me!" I roared.

He knew I wouldn't hesitate to sign anything dealing with money for my own gain! That muthafucka!

"I see he's been giving you strikes as well!" BJ laughed, pointing to the back of the folder. It read, STRIKE THREE! I just stood there and cried.

"I still have a couple more tricks up my sleeve! Are you with me or not?" BJ asked. Right when I was about to answer, my phone buzzed! The two hundred million dollars I stole from Ashton and Christian were withdrawn from the offshore account!

FUCK! I clicked on the image button and dropped my phone! "They know I killed them!"

"Killed who?"

"Our Grandparents!"

The picture was of the two medication bottles I used to poi-

222

son them! I hid them in their caskets!

"What's the plan?" I asked Billion. I hope it works this time because if not, I'll be dead next!

Chapter 36: Elanore and her Accomplices

"Be quiet! Yall gone, give us away with all that hackin!"

"Well, you know we have allergies! You got us in this pollinated maze! When is the last time somebody edged these muthafuckers up!" Celia complained!

"Maybe if you stop walking so close to them, you'll realize they are sculpted to perfection! Rose pressed!

"Are you sure this bitch took the bait? I'd hate to chase after her if she becomes aware of us before we get to her!" Celia fussed. "Yes, she took it! Linda was all too ready to jump on my husband's dick!" I revealed.

"To be honest, I'm surprised she came back after that harsh ass whoopin you gave her! Damn!" Rose commented.

I have to say, I never thought in a million years I would

see this bat again! When She tricked Victor into having sex with her, I lost a piece of my mind! I literally couldn't find it! I blacked out and beat the soul out of this woman! Linda did, however, take a secret with her.

"I know why she came back here, but I want you two to hear it from her slimy lips!"

Linda is one of those grimy bitches searching for the deepest pockets! After taking care of so many no-good men and being treated like shit. Linda decided she wanted to be a kept woman.

As we rounded the corner, Linda was naked, lying on the sitting bench. She was sunbathing, showing her pale ass to the clear blue sky!

"This bitch has no shame!" Celia whispered.

"It took you long enough! I got so hot, waiting!" Linda finally looked up and tried to cover up!

"What! What are you doing here?" Linda stuttered.

"I do believe I told you to NEVER come back here!"

"I just wanted Victor to know about his son!" She stood with a grin on her face!

"Let me get this straight, Linda! You come back after 35

years to tell somebody about a grown-ass man?" Rose asked.

"Yes! Victor needs to know about his son?"

"You do know Victor is an African American, right? And your son is a full-blooded Caucasian!"

Linda's eyes were as big as saucers.

"You thought you were going to share some news without producing the evidence! I did a blood test on ol' pinky when he fell out of your loose pussy! Turns out, you were a few weeks pregnant before you came up with that bullshit plan to trap, Victor!"

I'm still trying to figure out how she was going to pass a white boy off on Victor's black ass!" Rose quized, ans we all laughed!

"You black bitches think you know it all, don't you? Well, my son is going to have the last laugh! You won't even see him coming! We are going to take everything you own and laugh in your faces!" She boasted.

Linda tried to gather up some spit, but I busted her right in her mouth!

"Billion already tried to take our children from us and failed! Yeah, your sweet boy isn't as smart as he thought he was." I said to Linda as she struggled with her words.

"We know all about the plan to take over our land, Linda. I would tell you to warn your son, but something tells me you're not going to get that chance!"

Linda started to take in her surroundings.

"Aww! Hell, she looks like she's about to run yall!" Celia tied the laces on her shoes! And Rose stood in a football stance. Linda started screaming and running around in a circle!

"Help! These black bitches are trying to kill me!"

"Listen, Linda! NOBODY can hear your gullible ass!! We own this land also!"

None of us saw it coming! At least I didn't. Linda clipped her knee on the corner of the sitting bench. Sending her head-first into the cemented mermaid water fountain!

"DAMN! I was about to send this butterfly knife right through her dick suckers! She said black bitch one too many times for me!" Celia said.

"Ooh! That's nasty! Her clumsy ass killed herself!" Rose said, covering her eyes!

"WHAT THE HELL YALL BACK HERE DOING?" Red bellowed!

"YOU OLD FOOL, don't be sneaking up on me like that!

What's wrong with you?" Rose fussed.

"You've been moving funny, so I've been following you!" Red said, nonchalantly walking towards Linda's body.

"Damn, yall did a number on her!"

"WE DIDN'T DO SHIT! Her clumsy ass fell and killed herself!" Rose repeated.

"How did you know to take the left entry?" I questioned.

"There was a trail of M & M's leading me here!" Red admitted. I just shook my head because that was all Rose!

"What? I'm too cute to be lost in a damn maze!"

"Yes, you are!" Red said, dancing behind Rose!

"If you don't stop humping on me in front of them! They are going to think I don't give you any!"

"YOU DON'T!" Red yelled, defeated.

I called the clean-up crew and headed home! I know Red probably outed me to Victor, so I needed to be prepared for a longwinded talk. I walked into silence. Victor usually watches some kind of sports or reading the newspaper.

Tiptoeing further into the living room. I thought I was home free until I heard him set his glass down on the counter!

"Are you done being mad?" he asked, and I shook my head, yes!

"Go to the room!" Victor commanded!" Oooh, I'm in troublllle!!!!! I thought as I bit my lip and obeyed my husband!

Chapter 37: Landin Forest

**"W**hat' up, old man, why you call me over her in the middle of the afternoon?" I asked great grand Raymond.

"Watch my Great- Greats! I need to run an errand real quick!" I turned to see all the kids sitting on the couch with their tablets.

"How did you end up with the kids anyway?" I quizzed.

"Rose, your Mama, and Elanore went somewhere!"

"Where did they go?"

"Look, if I'd known you were going to ask all these questions. I wouldn't have cussed out the census guy earlier! Now I'll be back, damn!" he fussed.

As Raymond walked out the door. I saw Victorious pull up in Victor's Maybach. Sneaky asses.

"Well, kids, what do yall wanna do besides play on your

tablets?"

"We want some popcorn!" They all yelled at the same time.

"Coming right up!" I went in search of the popcorn and poured the red jar into the popper! I grabbed the little fancy plastic bowls, and the kids started chomping down on the buttery delight!

"Your head looks like a jelly bean with freckles on it! Hahahahahahaha!" MayLynn said to JR.

"Your head is shaped like a cantaloupe! You could be Caillou's twin sister!" JR. Countered. laughing his ass off.

"Both of yall got two big Ratatouille bucky beaver teeth!" Ashley yelped.

"Uncle Landin, you look like that guy that does flips in his videos! Chris brownie tumbler cakes!" Kyle laughed.

"Ha..." These kids are cracking me the fuck up! I looked at the clock, and about two hours had passed! I was about to text Great-Grand when he came moseying in the front door!

"Let me find out you and Victorious is messing with the neighborhood hot to trot lady around the corner!" I laughed!

"Whatever, I'm past grown! I've lived three adult lives! 30+30+30! You can't tell me shit!" Raymond bragged, doing the shake-them haters off dance!

"Why are the kids giggling and spinning around like that?" Raymond said, running off to the kitchen.

About five minutes later, he came back sweating and out of breath!

"LANDIN! Which container did you get the popcorn out of?"

"The red one, why?" I asked.

"OH! SWEET PEACHES! WE GOING STRAIGHT TO HELL! THESE KIDS ARE HIGH AS SHIT! What made you pick the red one? That jar is laced with weed! Negro, their parents, are going to kill you!" Raymond fussed while looking for the car keys.

"ME! This is YOUR POPCORN! Who mixes weed in the popcorn?"

"I do nigga! You better not snitch, or Red is going to put me in a home! WE GOTTA GET THESE KIDS OUT OF HERE! he shouted. "What does RED mean on a traffic light, Landin?"

"It means stop 3G! Maylynn answered with the cheesiest grin on her face!

I can't even move my feet as I take in the atmosphere! Not

only did the kids eat the popcorn! I did as well! Hell, I was about to go make some more! I turned to see Great-Grand snapping his fingers in my face, and I laughed my ass off!

"OH, HELL, NAW! YOU'RE HIGH TOO? I'm leavin!" I heard great-Grand say.

I slowly gathered myself and walked to the kitchen to get us some water and an ice bucket. I then grabbed some wash-cloths and dipped them in the ice water!

"Here, put these towels over your faces!" They did as I said, and they all started to calm down a little. I looked around for the popcorn, but Great-grand must have gathered the bowls and threw them away!

After the kids settled, they took naps leaving me to clean up. When I walked to the kitchen. There weren't any traces of popcorn, nor was there a trace of (G-G) Raymond! WOW!

"Hey! Baby, what are you doing here? You need to be some-where trying to work it out with your wife!" My mom said.

"Here we go! I came to check in on yall, but Great-Grand said he needed to run an errand and for me to watch the kids!"

"Where did that old goat have to go on a Saturday after-noon?" Red asked with an arched brow!

"Hey, yall, I just got back, and I'm going to go lay down!

Great-Grand appeared out of nowhere, then speed-walked to his room!

I bent over and clutched my stomach. That old man needs his own sitcom! I can not believe he pretended to never be here! When those kids wake up! It's a wrap for his ass

∞∞∞

I was still a little hungry, so I stopped to get soup and salad from Salata's. As I stood in line, I heard someone clear their throat.

"Hi, long time no see!" English smiled, and I disregarded her presence.

"So, you're really going to act like we weren't even a couple! You could at least say hello! Ignoring me is only pissing me off! I mean, now that you and Sage aren't together anymore! You can at least come by and talk to me now!" she sang while running her finger down the middle of her oily breast.

"Here you go, sir!" The cashier called out to me while giving English the side eye!

"Thank you!"

I walked out of the restaurant, thinking English would

leave me be!

"You'll be sorry, Landin. I swear you will!" English screamed at my back!

I needed some advice from Jaylin, so I stopped by his job. What I saw before my eyes mimicked an action   packed kungfu movie as my brother beat the hell out of five guys dressed in martial arts uniforms!

I pulled out my phone and recorded this shit! Before you even ask why I'm not helping. Jaylin doesn't like for people to jump into his fights. However, if you do, he will purposely tag your ass in the eye. That's just how he is!

Jaylin didn't even break a sweat. Suddenly a screaming female ran to help one of the guys who was unconscious. Did this nigga just pull out his phone and take a selfie with the dummies he just laid out? Jaylin is crazy as hell!

Chapter 38: Billion

"**I** don't need you to argue with me; I just want you to do what I tell you to do, English! Be at my apartment in 15 minutes!"

I've been fucking with English heavy since my love for chocolate left me! Terry has been missing in action, and all I can think about is her taste and smell!

Bella and English are like watered-down chocolate milk compared to Terry! They have the potential but lack the wholeness I needed. FUCK! I need Terry back!

After Bella told me she killed her grandparents! I've been looking at her differently! She is undoubtingly all about self! And right now, all I need are team players.

I hired five jujitsu masters to go and kick Jaylin's ass! Serves him right for how he did, Bella! One of the guy's girlfriends said she would record it live for me! I couldn't answer the video call quick enough!

As I watched my money go to fucking waste and listened

to the girl scream in my ear over her man's injuries. Another video came through my phone of the same fight but with commentary. I don't know the person's voice, but I could tell it was one of his brothers. This muthafucka even took a selfie after knocking them all out!

I began to think maybe I was in over my head!

"I'm here now what?" English said, uninterested in life. I gave her my phone, and she laughed!

"You idiot! Jaylin's been a master in jujitsu since 16 years old. Even Landin is a black belt! You really need to ask me before you go forward with your bright ideas!"

"Well, how about this? We go after their women next! Send them the full address to Hats. We can get them in a room and have some guys come and rough them up a bit!"

"That sounds like a great idea! I can't stand any of those bitches! They think they're better than me! I can't wait to see them helpless and in pain!"

I noticed faint marks on English's legs! But that didn't stop my mind from wandering all over her body! Plus, this Viagra pill just took effect! I ran my hands down to English's enormous ass, and she didn't have on panties! So, I slid my large fingers in between her folds. This is what I liked about English!

She got nice and wet with minimal effort!

I'm 6'2 236lbs. I don't have an extended package, but I know how to work it! My width makes up for the lack of length.

"You must not miss me too much if you're in here digging up in this broad's choocie!" Terry announced, walking through my bedroom door!

"Come sit on my face, and I'll show you how much I've missed you!

The three of us sexed each other for about three hours! I got excited, thinking about how I was going to get a victory soon! We showered and got to work on our plan. However, I couldn't help but noticed how Terry wasn't in accord with what English and I came up with!

"This is going to be a disaster! I can feel it! Terry confessed.

"Please don't tell me you've turned into a scary bitch all of a sudden! We are a lot stronger together than we are alone!" English sassed.

"English, you've been around those men just as long as I have! Do you honestly think they aren't going to tear that place up over their women? I mean this is the place where we make an obscene amount of money in one night, or did you forget? This could potentially shut Hats down, and I'm not trying to give up this fast money!" Terry countered.

I walked towards her and held her tightly!

"Soon, we aren't going to need to turn tricks anymore at Hats. We are going to be Billionaires!"

"I just sent the message to ILynn, Angel, and Sage! So, there's no turning back now! You're either in or out!" English snarled.

Terry sat down, pouting like a child. I didn't say anything because I didn't want her to leave me again.

"Just trust me, Terry. If this goes sideways, taking their homes will be our triumph! I promise."

Terry

I got the hell out of there as quickly as possible! I don't want to be a part of this shit any longer! After jumping out of Billion's car. I went home, packed a couple bags, and headed to a hotel right outside the city. In the middle of unpacking my second suitcase! I almost lost my bowls when I heard his voice!

"There's nowhere you can run, Terry," Major spoke calmly!

"I, please, I."

"Shhhhhhhhhhhh." Here's what you're going to do. You're going to stay here and play the part! Here are some things I want you to place in Billion's apartment! Once you've adjusted the items in the right areas. You will leave and meet me at the address I just sent to your phone!

I drove to my destination in fear! This could be my last day on earth! I definitely didn't mean to have sex with Billion and English! She's a fucking nut case! Her drive for revenge is going to end badly. Hell, who am I kidding? The things I've done recently are just as fucked up!

As I got out of the car, I took in the boorish chilling atmosphere!

"It took you long enough. Let's go inside." Major said, appearing out of nowhere.

The smell in this building was awful! It smelled of spoiled greens and smoldering New York trash!

"Have a seat." Major directed.

As soon as I sat down, Landin and Jaylin came into the room, followed by Ashton and Christian. Tears fell from my eyes without warning! Perspiration from my armpits started to seep through my shirt!

"Guilty birds cry and sing sweet sorrows. Especially when they know there are no tomorrows." Landin recited.

"Damn! Nigga I forgot you do poetry! That was cryptic but good, no less! Christian reassured.

"Tell us what we want to know, and don't leave anything out!" Christian said sternly. I sang like the songbird Landin said I was. I even shared shit that happened in high school they may not have known about!

"And tonight? What was discussed tonight?" They invited yall wives to the underground sex world at Hats! Billion wants to hurt them to get back at you for embarrassing him!" I confessed. I went on to tell them more, and they gave me orders; an informant agreed to obey.

Before I was able to walk out of the door. Landin asked me if I thought Billion would like a Hershey candy bar. He handed me what used to be Emery's tattoo in a plastic bag! I screamed and peed a little! Landin laughed at me then told me to beat it! These muthafuckas are too damn fine to be so mean!

All I could think about was if that was Emery back there, stinking! I mean, we haven't seen her in weeks. I really thought about taking my chances to run anyway. But what Major said about finding me! Sent chills down my spine!

Chapter 39: Angel Banks

"Christian is going to make me kill his ass! All up in a sex dungeon watching bitches twerk, uh! Well, he's about to see me whoop his ass all over that joint!" I yapped in ILynn's ear!

"You don't even know if that's what the text meant! You see, I'm not over here going nuts because I know damn well Major's muthafuckin ass ain't crazy enough to be down in a nasty sex dungeon!"

"So, are you not going with me tonight?" I asked,

"Fuck, yeah, I'm going! Are you crazy?"

"The invite says to wear a messy hair bun, a trench coat, thigh-high boots, and dark sunglasses! Did you call Sage to see if she's riding out with us?"

I feel so sorry for my girl! Although I thought she was stupid as hell for hiring a bitch to test her husband. I sincerely believe she's sorry about what she's done!

"She's not coming. She doesn't think she has a right to investigate his whereabouts. I told her she needs to fight for her marriage because Landin is really thinking about divorcing her." ILynn informed.

"All hell naw, Sage is coming even if I have to drag her ass out the bed! She is going to be present tonight. Let me get off of this phone, so I can get dressed." I hung up with ILynn and called Sage.

"Bring all of your clothing on the invite and get your ass over here now!" I yelled on the phone and hung up!

It took me an hour to do Sage's hair and make-up because she kept crying. After we finished dressing. I put Sage's butterfly clip in and made her twirl around in the mirror!

"That nigga better stop being stubborn! You better show him what he's going to miss tonight. If he ignores you, keep reminding him of your presence." I expressed.

Christian just arrived, so I took my trench coat off and told Sage to meet me at ILynn's house!

"Hey, babe!" I leaped up and kissed his chocolate lips!

"What's up? You smell good!" Christian kissed my neck.

"Where are you going babe, you just got here!" I tried my hardest not to pop his ass in the back of the head.

"I'm going to a new spot. Major and Landin turned me on to." Christian smiled slyly!

This muthafucka!

"Oh! Okay! Well, I'm going to take CJ to my Abuela's and head over to ILynn's house for lady's night!"

"You know you can ask me anything, right, Angel?"

"Yep! Have fun, and I'll see you in a bit, love!"

I made like the roadrunner and drove CJ to my Abuela's house! When I pulled into ILynn's driveway, she and Sage were walking out of the front door!

"Let's go! I just received a picture of them going into one of those backrooms!" ILynn panted!

"OH! Hell! Naw! Hold on to your necks!" I sped off, possibly giving them whiplash.

My heart pounded as smoke spewed out of my ears! All I saw was blood red!

"What's the password?" The voice said on the other side of the door!

"Flogger!" ILynn and I said at the same time! If I was a scary bitch I would have ran at the sight of this massive jolly green giant standing in the doorway!

In my overwrought state of mind! A four-headed dragon spitting fire couldn't stop me from running to the blue room! The guy offered to give us a tour, but we didn't need one! Don't ask me about the scenery of this place because I didn't give a fuck!

"I think the blue room is that way judging by the picture!" Sage said, seeming nervous.

We unclipped our butterfly barrette knives and took our position to slice off some nipples! ILynn pushed the door open, and my future hot flashes greeted me with a vengeance! I asked myself why didn't I just ask my husband that simple question; he said I could. "Fuck!"

Christian and Major were sitting in a chair, wiping their bloody knives off with handkerchiefs! Landin was standing off to the side on his phone! When I moved further into the room. I saw three tables with ropes hooked onto each side. There was also a broken movie camera sitting in the corner.

"What the hell!" I yelped when I saw where the trail of blood led to! ILynn had her hand over her mouth while Sage and Landin stared at each other intently! I was waiting for Christian to look at me when Auntie B came from the back of the room. She had a mini baby blue cooler and a black cooler!

"Bluuuuhhh!" ILynn gestured.

"Did yall know all those fools had green eyes? I've never been so lucky to collect that many in one night! Oh, hey, girls!"

I couldn't do anything but stare at Auntie B! She just plucked out some eyeballs for sport!

"Aww! ILynn, don't tell me you have a weak stomach! They're just eyes!" She held the yeti up like it contained diamonds. I don't even wanna know what was in the other cooler!

Auntie B laughed as she packed up the rest of the things from the back! Hell. I was still waiting for my husband to look at me! That's how I know he's pissed!

"Have a seat." He says. Shit, here we go!

"What's the first thing you agreed to do when you hear something about me from an outside source?"

I just put my head back on the chair! I could answer him, but I'm not! I'm stubborn as hell.

"Oh, you're not going to answer me?" he said now standing.

"If yall received this text and this picture, the response would be the same!" ILynn interrupted.

"A simple question should have been the only option! Instead, yall wanna gear up and play inspector gadget! And I don't even know why you came here with them! I'm not fuckin with you like that!" Landin spouted.

"Bruh!" Major added.

"Naw! Go ahead and tell them what the fuck could have happened to them!" Landin yelled towards our direction.

"This was a setup! You three were about to be brutalized and humiliated on camera. One of our most notorious enemy's offspring sprang up a plan to tear out our heartbeat. I keep waiting for you all to get it through your thick skulls. We gotta be elite with our thinking and actions! And, ILynn, I'm disappointed because you knew what it was when you walked across that bridge!" Major expressed.

"Auntie B, can you please see that Kiley's Butterfly Killers get home safely?" Christian asked.

We didn't say shit! We just followed Auntie B out of a side door on the other side of the room! Knowing I should have responded better. I'll just take this shit with a grain of salt and my dildo. Because I know this man is going to withhold the dick as punishment.

Chapter 40: Major Forest

People should really pay more attention to their surroundings. I sat in the corner of Terry's hotel room for thirty minutes, watching her unpack her clothes. I thought about ending her but figured she'd be a good asset for now! I gave her translucent stickers to put throughout Billion's home!

I needed to know this bastard's every move! The fact that we've been under surveillance for five years has me unrest! We need to make sure to destroy all the incriminating evidence he has on the judge. Killing Billion before then could lead to the Elite's exposure!

Terry informed us about the pictures Jamie had taken and copied to a hard drive. She then pleaded to confiscate the copies for us. As if she had a choice. I almost felt sorry for how she was roped into all of this. But deceit is deceit! Besides, she's a fucking thief and needs to be taught a lesson.

I laughed so hard when Landin threw Emery's skin tattoo at her! Terry literally pissed her pants! I wanted Terry to come there so she could smell and wonder if that was Emery's stench in the air! For now, I'll let her think that's where she'll end up.

However, Emery and a few others have been moved to a more nutrient territory! (Yes, I meant nutrient.). Christian and Landin couldn't believe Emery was the chick he had a date with a few years ago! Once we figured out her tattoo was her original skin color. She sang like those songbirds Landin talks about.

"I'll tell you everything. Just please don't kill me! It all started with Jamie telling BJ who you all were! She didn't know much, though! BJ seemed to have apprehended more information about you all than she did. Jamie informed him of English, which was a whole new monster! Her hunger for revenge against Landin attracted him.

They found me in Germany! A lady named Nadia, Billion, and English lived there for a whole year, gathering up soldiers to take you all down. That's when I came into the picture. Before I knew it, they were going to kidnap me, but I went willingly. I'd hit rock bottom and didn't want to disappoint my parents.

Listen, I'll do anything! I'll even give you the money I made off of deceiving Christian and Landin! Landin immediately grabbed her phone and made her put in her information! And just like that! $800,000 went into the "No More Homeless Families Organization fund!"

Landin promised her he would put her name on a plaque stating the amount of her donation! All that scheming and agreeing to fuck up people's marriages. Turned into helping real people who need it! I don't know what will happen to Emery. But I'm sure somebody has something in mind!

I really thought ILynn was going to tell me about the invite she'd received. She fucked up when she asked me what I was about to get into as soon as I walked into the house! She's never asked me that before. I figured ILynn was too hyped so, I gave her the same little speech Christian gave Angel! You see, that shit didn't work!

Christian, Landin, and I spotted Jamie as soon as we walked into the room. The expression on her face was priceless! Her Dom or master smacked her hard with the flogger so loud that it was heard across the room!

As we took in our surroundings and persons in attendance. Terry informed us of which room housing the men hired to violate our women would be in.

All I could see was darkness! We had Terry stash weapons in the room! With all the training and simulation tests. They wouldn't have stood a chance. It was seven guys the size of linebackers in that room! I'm sure the ladies would have sliced and diced those niggas up, but not enough to avoid being apprehended.

In my state of darkness, pillars of men fell to their knees! The angst and pain caught in their throats gave me great satisfaction. As I came to, three of the seven men's chests were face down on the floor with their faces staring back at me! Landin and Christian both had two men, a piece lying on the floor in front of them!

It was a bloody mess due to Christian and Landin cutting off fingers and tongues! I thought it was overkill but to each his own. I can't even say I was surprised to see Auntie B sashaying into the room with her Eagle claw coolers! Christian stood there with his mouth open the whole time as she collected her jewels!

However, when she got to slicing off the other jewels, we dragged the men to the back of the room. We didn't wanna see that shit!

We sat and waited for the ladies to arrive. Landin didn't think Sage would come because of their current situation! But I know he still loves her; she just cut him deep with this one.

When ILynn busted in here, Angel said, who's ready to get

their nipples sliced off! I almost forgot how pissed I was that ILynn's sexy ass came through the door with the newbie attire on. That fucking trench coat and thigh highs is to let all of the Doms know there's fresh meat in the building!

Them trying to act hard and not apologize only pissed me off more! I got something for that, though! But first, I need to send a little message!

Me: "You missed muthafucka!"

Chapter 41: Jamie Winters White

I can't get Major out of my mind! I tried so hard, and for a while, I thought I was completely over him! That night at Hats, I was fighting so hard not to give in to my orgasm! Sonny had been giving it to me so good! However, when Major's sexy dominant in his own right walked through! My water dam broke!

"Did you just cum after you laid eyes on that man?"

"I'm sorry!" is all I could say in my awestruck state!

"Let me go, Jamie!"

I still had Sonny in a vice grip and couldn't let go! My pussy contracted over and over, watching Major move throughout the room!

Those lashes Sonny was giving me with his flogger only made it worse! As he tried to pull out of me! I could feel him getting angry! A dominant wants to be the only reason for your ecstasy! It's an ego thing, I know, but I agreed to it!

Sonny went into the wash-up rooms while I tried to figure

out why Major, Christian, and Landin just walked in here like they owned the place! All the Dom's put together couldn't compare to these men! Out of my peripheral, I saw a woman snap a picture of them!

This Woman looked awfully like my cousin Amber! But I knew damn sure this bitch wouldn't show her face in this town again! Let her tell it some bad people were after her and her mother for money!

I was about to go be nosey until Three bad bitches walked through the door! Taking a closer look, I could tell it was ILynn, Angel, and Sage! What the fuck is going on, I thought as I took care of my hygiene in the other washroom! All of them being here is no coincidence! This has English and Billion written all over it!

"Let's go. We're done here!" Sonny grabbed my arm and led me towards the exit! I don't know what's gotten into him, but I'll obey for now!

The suspense is killing me, though! "Sonny, you need to stop handling me like this! You have a wife at home! How do I know you're not thinking about her when you're inside me?

"Shut the fuck up, Jamie! You're just trying to deflect what you did back there! You never came that hard with me before, and you expect me to sweep it under the rug! Naw, you need to be taught a lesson!" Sonny said in anger!

"What would that be? It's not like your wife will be up for a fuck session! She's a drunk, remember!" I screamed in his face!

∞∞∞

I sat in my room and cried as Sonny made love to his wife! I didn't know what changed her routine in the past three months of being here. But Tammy was hot and ready for her husband as soon as we stepped in the door!

I have a hunch that my being here sparked a little fire alerting Tammy of her shortcomings! Hell, there is no way I would allow another female to stay with my husband and me. My attack taught me not to trust anyone!

I eased up to Sonny and Tammy's bedroom and slightly opened the door! Sonny's sex drive is wild! He could cum several times and still be rock hard! I watched him move in and out of Tammy's drunk pussy!

She was pushing him away if he went too deep! Weak bitch! Tammy shook violently and made the ugliest face before she passed out, out from her first orgasm. Just as I thought, Sonny was still rock hard and unsatisfied! He tried thumbing with her clit to wake her up, but she started snoring!

It irritated me that I made Sunny feel this way. But, he knew the history of how I felt about Major! Major is the only thing I haven't conquered, and it killed me! Why won't he just give me a chance to hop on it? I had to shake myself out of my delusion!

"Get the fuck out of my room, Jamie!"

I hadn't noticed I was still standing in their doorway! My feelings were hurt at how Sonny spoke to me! A sense of regret came over me, and that too was very foreign. As I made my way back to the guest bedroom. I began to pack.

"What are you doing, Jamie?" Sonny asked, standing behind me.

"I'm leaving you! This is not right! I'm going back home to my family!

"Please, baby, don't leave! It pissed me off to know Major made you cum like that while I was inside of you!" Sonny led me to the guest shower and proceeded to wash my whole body!

My addiction lit a fire so hot we both could have caught on fire!

"OOOOhhhhh! Sonny's tongue slow danced with my clit! I rained on his tongue as forbidden thoughts of Major resurfaced!

"Don't you think it's too late to be singing in the shower?" Tammy slurred from the door of the guest bathroom.

Sonny halted all movement as I removed my leg off of his shoulder!

"Oh! I'm sorry, did I wake you!"

"Yes, as a matter of fact, you did! Have you seen my husband?"

"No, not since he picked me up from work. Is everything okay!" I asked, now concerned at her tone.

"No! You being here is a concern! You know I'm not crazy! I could have sworn I heard you in my room! Sonny says I was dreaming, but I know what I heard! You want my husband, don't you, Jamie?" she taunted.

You're the student he fucked and made crazy, aren't you? I heard all of the rumors! You need to get the fuck out of my house this instant! Fucking bitch! You've been in here fucking my husband right under my nose, haven't you?"

I was fucking speechless! Tammy was relentless, so I decided to push my luck.

"Yes, we fucked in your bed while you were sleeping. You

drunk skunk! We fucked all over that room while whole bottles of wine coursed through your body!" I spat, but wasn't finished.

"You see, Sonny figured you loved Cabernet Sauvignon better than him, so he went out and got a Marlot!" Tammy reared back and slapped the hell out of me! When she struck me, flashes of my mother fluttered before me!

"Fuck!" I hollered!

"Are you okay, baby?" Sonny fret concerned, not realizing he'd just fucked up!

"What the fuck! So you've been in here the whole time? You fucking bastard!" she screamed.

Tammy was trying her hardest to beat the hell out of Sonny! He blocked her every attempt, which infuriated her even more! Tammy turned to leave the bathroom when she fell face forward onto the ground!

Sonny and I sat there for hours, thinking about how lucky we were! The paramedic told us Tammy seemed to have had a heart attack!

Ching! Ching! I thought, but this shit was intangible! I was leaning more towards poisoning her beloved wine. All I could think about was how Sonny and I could live happily out in the open now!

Chapter 42: Jaylin Forest

I walked into work finding my employees, hovering over the security monitors.

"What are you all looking at?"

"We're looking at a ninja whoop these dudes' asses with no effort at all!"

Shit! I forgot to delete that footage!

"Bossman, you gotta show me those moves!" Allen commented.

"Hell, yeah! Bossman!" The others agreed.

"I'll think about it," I assured. Trolling to my office, I heard someone sniffling.

"Oh! My Gosh, Mr. Forest, I didn't know you were coming in today!" Vina wiped her eyes!

I don't know what the fuck my heart just did, but I ignored it! Lately, I've felt like Vina belonged to me.

"Why are you crying?" I asked.

"It's noting I can't handle." Vina tried to brush it off!.

"That's not what I asked you, Vina. Come here." She walked towards me, somewhat timid and afraid.

"My ex is threatening to post a video of us having sex! I'm petrified that my parents and sisters will see it!"

Vina handed me her phone with the video still playing on mute. I instantly became furious! I sent the recording to Major with special instructions.

"Everything will be fine! Dry your tears. I'll handle everything!" I didn't realize I was holding her to my chest! Letting her go made my heartache!

"I don't want you to get involved in my bullshit, Mr. Forest! You have a beautiful wife and son to look after." She concluded.

"I have a son to look after, and Bella is no longer my wife. Your bullshit became mine when I realized you were reading to Jr. on facetime. And please call me Jaylin" Vina was rendered speechless.

For the past few weeks, I would here, Jr. cracking up after I'd tucked him into bed! I should have known something was a little off when he told me he didn't need me to read to him anymore! Jr. loves it when I read to him before bed so, his confession left me a little salty.

After hearing Jr. giggle one time too many! I marched to his bedroom to see what was so funny. Vina's voice carried through the air sending waves of joy to my soul! Jr. had admiration, love, and comfort in his eyes as he watched her on his phone!

I spent the rest of the day preparing for everyone to be underground! I had extra cameras and mics placed in everyone's homes!

Although my brothers and I don't plan on returning to our current residents, we left the furniture, beds, and a few art pieces. Just to give them the aspect of violating our spaces.

I called Justin back here from New York to run the office while diligently retrieving important information. Besides, Justin will know what to do if Bella tries to come up here to reclaim some shit! I could only imagine how pissed she was being tricked into signing divorce papers.

Dame, Uncle Dom's brother, is head of the police department! He informed us that tomorrow he would be issuing the fake warrant for us to vacate the property! We need this to look as authentic as possible.

Needing a moment to myself. I sent everyone home early!

"Are you ready for this bullshit? Landin asked from the doorway.

"I can't wait until this shit is over with! Are you prepared to be down there with Sage? You are going to have to talk to her sooner or later, Landin.

"I'm more concerned with all the questions the kids are going to have!" We both laughed.

"What do you think about Vina?" I asked Landin.

"When I said she would be a perfect match. I didn't actually mean for this job but for you! I know it was a fucked up thing to do, not really aware of what was going on with you and Bella.

It just felt right to introduce you to her. Vina instantly gave me Sister-in-Law vibes when I met her."

"I kind of want to feel her out a little bit before I make a move! I need to get this right this time! Bella is a deadbeat!

This morning I caught Vina in here crying. She said her ex is blackmailing her with a sex tape!! I called Major, so he could hack into his phone and computers. That nigga is going to wish he never met her!" I stressed, gripping the edge of my seat!

"You should probably go get her! There's no telling how long we are going to be in the bunker.

I thought about how Vina was going to react when I commanded her to come with me. I can't leave her behind. Not with my ex, or hers for that matter. Threats almost always turn physical sooner or later. Ding Dong! I rang Vina's doorbell.

"Hey! Mr. I mean Jaylin! What are you doing here? Did I forget to do something?

My lips crashed into hers with a vengeance! I picked her tall, thick frame up as she wrapped her legs around my waist! I pressed her up against the nearest wall while she unbuttoned my shirt! Our tongues danced real slow, and our hearts tempo did the Rumba!

She screamed in shock at my fulfillment, and her thunderstorm peaked unembarrassed. At least that's what played in my mind while staring at her luscious lips! Fuck! Get it together nigga! "Jaylin, are you alright! Do you need to come in?" Vina asked, concerned.

Vina's house was beautifully decorated in soft grays and about three different shades of greens and oranges. The deep gray hardwood floors were pleasantly clean with a scent of vanilla in the air! Vina's decorating skills were up there with my sister-in-law. She had a dining room table that fit six people and a big ass shaggy dog making its way to me.

"Do you trust me, Vina?" I asked, trying not to scare the shit out of her.

"Yes! I trust you, Jaylin." She confessed.

"I need you to pack a suitcase with maybe seven changes of clothes. I have to leave, and I'm not going without you! I'll explain everything on the way to my house."

I was expecting Vina to tell me to get out or think this was all a joke, but she didn't! She just retreated to her bedroom! 30 minutes and two suitcases later! Vina was ready to go! I informed my parents and grandparents of our guests. Needless to say, Landin beat me to it! We dropped her dog off at her parent's house. I could tell she had questions.

Vina's parents are both Doctors, and she is the oldest of 6 siblings. Four girls, two boys. Vina sings in her church choir, and she teaches ballet at the performing arts institute. If I'd been paying attention, I would have noticed she was one of the performers at the Excellence Ball five years ago!

"Does any of this have something to do with those men you beat down in the parking lot?" "What I'm about to tell you can't be repeated in any way! I have strong feelings for you, Vina.

And I hope you will be around for a long time! But if you repeat what I'm about to tell you. I'll be ordered to kill you!

Do you still want to go with me?"

"Yes."

Chapter 43: The quickies

Ashton & Kiley

"Baby, you know we need to be down there in like 15 minutes!!!! Fuuuuuuuuuuuuuuuuck Kileyyyyyyy!!!! Ahhh-hhhh! Shiiiiiiiiiiittttttt!" "Mommy, are you in there tickling Daddy again!"

Major & JLynn

Smack, smack, smack, smack!!!! Uh Uh Uh, Uh, Oooooooooohhhhh! Ssssssss! Smack! WAP, WAP, WAP, WAP, WAP! "RIGHT THERE MAJORRRRRR-RRR!!!!! FALSETTO!!!

BANG! BANG! BANG! "Daddy! What are you in there doing to my momma! She's singing as loud as she can! Don't you smack her anymore, or I'm going to tell Nana on you!" MayLynn said through the door!

"GO BACK TO BED, MAYLYNN!" We both yelled!

Christian & Angel

"Damn! Angel, you're wet as fuuuuuuuuuuuuck!" "Oh! Yeah! CHRISTIAN! OH MY GOD!!!!!!!!! Go, FASTERRRRRRR-RRR!"

"AAAAAAUUUUUNNNNGGGGGGG!!!! Baby, I think I just got you pregnant with three sets of twins!"

"SIX BABIES! OH NO! LORD, PLEASE DON'T' DO ME LIKE THAT!" Angel and I heard CJ. Yell through the door!

Red & Rose

 Ain't shit going on here! NEXT Chapter, please!"

Chapter 44: The Bunker

Rose

This old man is driving me insane! I had to go get the blue pill for women! However, my prescription wasn't ready until this afternoon. "Look at your husband over there in the corner, talking to himself!" Bobbye chuckled!

"He'll be alright! I got something for that later on!" I stuck my tongue out like that little Cardi B does!

"Ugh!" B turned her lip up and walked off! She's hilarious!

"What's wrong with you, pretty little girl?" I asked May-Lynn.

"Nanna Rose? Did you bring your stick with you?"

"No, why would I need my stick, Maylynn?" I asked, concerned.

"My momma was trying her hardest to sing and couldn't! Daddy was smacking her a lot, and she got louder and louder and louder! Then her voice cracked, and that's when I heard more smacking!"

Oh! This little girl is going to be the death of me! "I marched right to that door and said stop smacking my mommy, or I'm going to tell my Nanna Rose!" I looked around to see if anyone was listening to her! I'm going to die laughing!

"CJ. Why are you pouting like that, babycakes? "My parents are going to make me become an older brother six times at the same time! So, in nine months! I'm going to be moving in with Nanna Ella and Grandpa Sr."

This shit is too funny!

"OH! MY! GOODNESS! DID YOU SEE THAT?" MayLynn shouted, grabbing my hand and leading me to Celia and Ru-momd!

"You should've brought your stick, Nanna!"

Celia

Love, money, pussy, and pain can blind a man's judgment. The aura of despair is all over my son Landin. Times like this, I wish I could make it better, but I have to let him figure it out.

"Baby, Landin is stubborn, just like your ass, and I'm tired of seeing him do this to himself," I said to Rumond.

"The fuck you bring me into this for? I'm sitting here, minding my own business, playing this **Boojee Babies Bingo** you got me hooked on!" Rum responded.

"You know! For you to be a judge, you have an alarming potty mouth!"

"You don't have any complaints when I...."

"RUM!" I yelped as he smacked me hard on my backside!

Out the corner of my eye, I could see MayLynn and Momma Rose headed in our direction!

"Did you just smack my Grandma Celia on her bottom, Rum Pop?" she asked with her black eyes bulging and her hands on her hips!

"Uh! Somebody better come get this little girl!" Rum shouted.

"Get him, Nana Rose! And then you gotta go get my daddy for smacking my mommy over and over because she can't sing!"

"MAYLYNN! Get your little ass over here! We need to have a long talk!" ILynn snapped at her daughter!

"That's right! You better get her before I do?" Rum countered. "Did yall see that shit?"

Momma Rose, Rum, and I laughed so hard! MayLynn is going to give them hell! It's going to be crazy down here in this bunker with this bunch!

I watched my family make their way down here! There's nothing in this world I wouldn't do for them! I'm also proud we are here in one piece! This pale muthafucka gotta go! Got me down in this bunker! Like we're running from the terminator or something!

Victorious

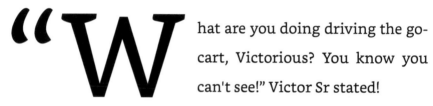

"**W**hat are you doing driving the go-cart, Victorious? You know you can't see!" Victor Sr stated!

I'm driving this muthafucka to the other end of the bunker so I can watch TV!" Shit, I almost gave myself up just then! I got this new weed that turns me into a blabbermouth!

"Let me drive you down there!" Sr. said, trying to grab the keys!

"I will bite your damn hand off! Get away from me; I can still see and drive! Hell, I've been driving your Maybach around town for months! Oh, shit!" Ella laughed, and I just pressed on the gas as Sr. turned three different shades of black! With his black ass!

Look at this old fart, thinking he's too cool for school! "Who you texting Cool Mo D?" Just then, my phone buzzed!

I just shook my head! "You couldn't just say it to me? I'm sitting right in front of you!" I said to Raymond. Well, I didn't see your light, bright ass sitting in that go-cart! Hell, yall the same damn color beige nigga!" This fool going blind for real! I am pecan brown.

"How did they get the kids down here?" Raymond asked.

"They were all sleep until they laid them down," I responded.

"Those little slicksters were probably faking!"

"Oh! Look at that beauty Jaylin just brought down here!" Ray grinned.

"You haven't even seen her face yet! She could have a pug face!" We both laughed

When that girl took off her blindfolds, I fell in love! "Daaa-aaaaaaaaaaaaaaammmmmmnnnn! Let's go, say hi!" We sped off in their direction!

"Whoa! What kind of motor did yall put in this go-cart?" Jaylin spouted.

"Vina, you remember the great-greats of the family!" Jaylin

announced,

"Oh, this is Vina from your job! You're Regina's great-grand-daughter! She was fine as hell! If I hadn't fallen in love with Ivy, I probably would have been your Great-Grand!" We all laughed.

Vina

When Jaylin knocked on my door, I tried hard not to fall in his arms! The weakness I feel in my knees when I see him is ridiculous. Jaylin strongly reminds me of the Late Great Nipsey Hussle. His persona also made me feel protected and held with high regard!

Jaylin asked me if I trusted him, and I said yes without hesitation. So, when he put the blindfold around my eyes, I wondered why he didn't return the gesture. Jaylin summarized what I needed to know about his family. I'm sure I should run, but I don't think he would let me!

I must have fallen asleep. I woke up to Jaylin carrying me inside a humungous building! I couldn't help my attraction to him! I wanted to ask so many questions. I wanted to know how Bella could leave Jaylin and her child behind?

I was still curious about why he wanted me to come here. The two older gentlemen I made popcorn for almost ran us over with this high-speed go-cart! When Victorious mentioned my great-grandmother, I was in a fit of laughter.

I can't say I didn't already know who Victorious was! My Great-grand talked about him all the time after his wife passed and her second husband died. She would talk about how all the girls wanted Victorious, but he only had eyes for Ivy!

I was so overwhelmed with the love his family had been giving me! It's like I'd belonged here or that they were waiting on me to arrive home from a long trip. "Hey! Sister-in-Law, it's good to see you again!" Kiley cheered.

"Aw, yeah, you're a winner if the sister likes you! Kiley is bat shit crazy over her brother's!" Raymond announced.

Kiley just shook her head. We could hear arguing between Landin and Sage before Junior ran up to me and gave me a big hug!

"Hi! Miss Vina, the ballerina!" Junior sang loudly!

Before I knew it, all of the kids were hugging me!

"A real-life ballerina! That's what I wanna be when I grow up!" Ashley professed. "You must be the tooth fairy or something with the way they all just ran over here!" Red joked.

All this love made me feel like a legit superstar!

"Miss Vina, can you sing me to sleep?" Junior pleaded.

"Well damn, she can sing too! Where you been hiding all these years! I know for sure Jaylin wouldn't have married that hot Cheeto if he'd seen you first!" Red informed.

"Red, leave her alone before you scare her off! Besides, I got some candy in the room!" Rose teased.

Red made a sound very close to Scooby-Doo, and everybody laughed! This man practically ran to their room! After I sang, the kids to sleep, and their parents carried them off to bed. Jaylin gave me a tour!

"Whoever built this place is a genius!"

"Please don't say that too loud! Raymond will talk both your ears off!" Jaylin warned. I wouldn't mind hearing what the inspiration was for building this place."

"Well, in that case!" We heard Raymond behind us!

Kiley

"Landin! You need to calm down! We heard yall way down there! What were yall arguing about anyway!" I asked, wanting to know what possibly made them forget the kids were down here! For Landin to raise his voice means something fucked up is about to come out of it! I was glad Kelly was distracted by Vina's arrival!

Kelly is a different kind of child! She reminds me of Major! Mysterious, but very alert!

"Kelly's not stupid, you know! She going to call yall on this bullshit front yall think is under control!"

"Shit! Kelly called us on our bullshit a week ago! I'm so irritated I can't think straight! Everybody thinks it's so easy to work this shit out, but I feel so broken and meaningless. Like my word ain't shit!

Do you realize I was set up by my own fucking wife! Fuck! I can't even look at her without wanting to strangle her ass!"

I never in my life saw my brother cry! That shit did something to my soul! I had to show restraint and a lot of fucking patience!

I love Sage, and I want them to work this shit out! But this broken soul before me is weary.

"What was the argument about?" This nut came at me like a damn hurricane asking me if I was fucking English! I saw English last week while I was getting food!

She must have sent Sage some text messages lying about us sleeping together. I ignored her and continued to get the room ready. When I pulled the queen-sized beds apart, Sage flipped the fuck out! Talking about, she's still my wife and that I'm a horrible person for sleeping with Emery and English!"

"Wait! You didn't tell Sage you didn't sleep with Emery?

Landin

After Kiley gave me the business about not telling Sage the truth about what happened between Emery and me! I tried to look at it from her point of view. Serves her right to be in suspense! She started this bullshit in the first place!

Sage and I received text messages on our burner phones, telling us my father would mediate us in the morning! I knew that little spat got his attention, and my mother put her foot down.

I sat across from sage with a heavy heart! I could tell she had been crying all night! Just like all of the other nights, I watched her. I became curious! Why so much pain? Why is she hurting so much when this is all her fault! My mom walked in and sat next to Sage. And my father sat next to me!

"I want you both to know we are not in favor of this divorce. "We will, however, support you all either way! Who wants to go first?" My father asked.

"Landin, I tell you I'm sorry every day, and you ignore me! It was a mistake!" I sighed at those words!

"A mistake is like misspelling a word! Not going out and hiring a whole scheming bitch to seduce their husband!" I yelled.

"It's not your turn Landin." My pops said.

"I've been in love with you since we were children! I saw you run through different females like Usain Bolt's black ass." I would have laughed at that corny shit if I weren't pissed.

You've slept with two women while being married to me! I know I pushed the first one on you, but English?"

"What the hell, Landin! You didn't tell her the truth about what happened? My mom screeched.

"Why should I have told her the truth? This muthafucka set me up to fail and had divorce papers already drawn up and signed! You basically said fuck this marriage! And spit on my word.

You could've and should've come and talked to me! Your mind was made up, and it wasn't shit nobody could do or say about it! And for that! I'm going to give you what you want! Give me a pen!"

Sage grabbed the pen and threw it across the room! I got up

to get it when I heard Miss Alice in my ear!

"You have an altering task that will test your spirit. Be careful; it's deeper than you think! Her actions were taught,"

I didn't realize my back was up against the wall, and Sage had me in a gripping death hug!

"Why did you do it, baby?" i asked out of breath.

Sage explained the best way she could between tears! I didn't know any of this about her aunt!

My parents left the room while Sage and I talked it out most of the day!

"What made you ask why I did it, Landin? It seemed like you had an epiphany!"

"I actually did have one! It was something Miss Alice said to me! She works at the...."

"Chocolate Cup Coffee Shop!" Sage finished my sentence!

"Miss Alice warned me not to do this, but it was too late! I didn't remember until I was crying on the bathroom floor." Sage revealed.

Jaylin

We, as grown-ups, should be ashamed of ourselves listening at the door of the conference room! That is until we heard moaning and things being knocked off the tables!

"What are yall over here doing?" Victorious asked while zooming toward us in the go-cart!

"Oh, nothing, we all scattered! Victorious must have heard what we'd heard because he sped off laughing! I turned around, and Vina and Great-Grand had their shame fingers motioning! (G.G) Raymond held Vina hostage all night talking about this place!

I couldn't tell her everything! Not yet, at least! She nor the kids know about the several torture chambers in the south wing! I had it sealed off for our brief stay down here. All the kids are dressed and ready to jump into the Olympic size pool!

"Uncle Jay, where's my mom and dad?" Kelly asked.

"They're in there, making you a brother or sister!" May-

Lynn answered, walking past with her beach towel wrapped around her tiny body.

Major and ILynn must have had to talk to her about what she heard during their quickie session!

I couldn't even look at Kelly's small shocked face! She had a look of horror, and then she said,

"I guess that's okay! I'll still be the oldest and the one in charge! Just like you, Uncle Jay!"

"Yep, it's fun being in charge!" I assured.

"Look at this action figure, trying to see what we're over here talking about! He's been watching us all morning. Go ahead and tell him you don't want him. You want me now!" Great-Grand boasted, grinning ear to ear!

"Three G! you can't take my new mommy! I'll find you an old woman to talk to on that silver fox dating app." Junior announced. His comment took everybody out with laughter!

"What the hell is a silver fox? Did this little dude just call me a silver fox!" Raymond asked, leaning up in his chair.

"Come talk to me," I whispered in Vina's ear.

I laughed at how her body became flushed! If I make her feel like this, just talking to her. I wonder how her body will react when I devour her creamy chocolate center!

"Sure." She breathlessly responded.

"This place is really amazing! I can't imagine going back to my drab ol house after this!

It's like I'm in one of those design your dream home games! There is a whole grassland area with the illusion of being out-side!" She announced.

I unceasingly stared at her lips as she spoke with admir-ation! My burner rang with Dame's name displayed on it! Ex-cusing myself to answer, I kept my eyes on Vina. "It's time," Dame confirmed.

Because I didn't want everyone hauling ass to the media room. I gave Major a head nod to inform them. I already had the media room set up with food and drinks. I even grabbed some of Great-Grand's special popcorn he now hides in the shed!

"I'm sorry, Vina, I have to go..." I said, hating to be away from her any longer.

"Oh, no, go ahead, don't mind me! I'll go hang with the kids. Vina assured.

I wanted to ease the dubious glare she had in her eyes, but time waited for no one. I kissed her on her forehead and walked away!

"You better watch out, Miss Vina, my uncle, is going to put a baby in your stomach soon!" I heard MayLynn say!

"MAYLYNN!" Major yelled! And she ran as fast as she could towards her cousins. I didn't even see her tiny ass sneak up behind me!

Once everyone was seated, I pushed play to watch all the bullshit unfold.

"I can't wait to haunt those idiots! Great-Grand said to Victorious!

It was like a light bulb went off in my head! However, I couldn't address my suspicions. So I'll deal with it later!

Chapter 45: Billion and his little evictors

**"W**hat the fuck do you mean they're not home!"

I had my crew here to film the humiliation bestowed on their black faces!

"We've knocked on all the addresses listed! I assure you no one is at any of those addresses.

Bella turned the doorknob to her former house, and it was unlocked!

"Yeah, something isn't right because Jaylin never leaves the door unsecured."

"Well, you guys, go ahead! I'm going to head on over to Landin's house!" English then took off down the street!

Yeah, go on. I'll be down there later!" I assured.

I'm going to fuck her all over that house as well! We walked in, and Bella had the nastiest look on her face.

"Why would you be down there later?" she asked

"I wanna see inside everyone's house! Is that okay with you?"

I had to think of something quick! Lately, I've been slipping, not giving a damn about what I say! Now that I've breached this so-called powerful family! I don't really need Bella anymore.

"Where do you wanna fuck first?"

Bella

Billion's been acting really stressed out, but I've been handling that for him every day!I hope he doesn't think I'm blind to how he's been staring at Terry's ass. I sware I'm going to kill them both if their fucking behind my back.

I led Billion over to the couch, Jaylin and I picked out after our honeymoon! As I waited for Billion to sit down, I noticed the hand-stitched throw ILynn made us was gone, along with the accent pillows.

My panties being snatched off brought me back to reality and confusion at the same time! Billion has never been the aggressor when we had sex! He bent me over the couch and entered me carelessly!

"What are you doing!" I said, out of breath. Billion was going so fast I thought he was going to have a heart attack! I tried to rise up, and he pushed me back down and pulled my hair!

"Owww!" I cried, and he stopped.

"Get up, Cry, baby!"

I had to do a double-take at Billion's brash behavior!

"I'm sorry, I just got carried away! Come on, You can ride my face in yall bed! I was so excited! Billion watched my naked bouncy ass as we walked quickly through the hallway!

Billion hopped onto the California king-sized bed while I crawled to him!

"Hurry up, Bella, I got shit to do! I was yet again shocked by how he was treating me! I sat on his face, and he relentlessly went after my engorged button!

I couldn't speak. I was in a trance! Soon after, I saw stars and then total darkness!

English

I practically ran to Landin's house! There was absolutely no trace of me in this house whatsoever. I helped Landin pick out every piece of furniture, dishes, and picture art for his walls!

As I walked through the house, I became furious! Landin had gotten rid of everything I'd chosen for him! I didn't realize I'd fell to the floor in agony! My heart broke while I took in my surroundings.

I jumped up and stalked off to their bedroom!

"OH MY GOD!" I rolled around in their gorgeous silver fiberglass bed and pleasured myself.

I got myself so spent, I didn't realize Billion was standing in the doorway!

"I see you got started without me!" Billion climbed on the bed and went under the sheet! When his mouth latched on to my juicy nectarine, I closed my eyes and imagined he was Landin! Billion was making me feel so good, I had to bite my tongue hard, to provoke Landin's name from leaving my lips.

After countless rounds of revenge sex, I laid there in Landin's bed, wondering where they could possibly be? It's summer, so they could be on a family vacation!

"Hey, where are their clothes? I went to every room, and none of the clothes or shoes are in the closet and drawers." Billion announced, concerned.

"I think they're on vacation. Calm down!"

"Who the hell takes all of their clothes on vacation, English?"

I grabbed the top of Billion's basketball shorts and eased them down! I swallowed him whole, so he would shut the fuck up! Just as Billion's head went back and his mouth dropped open. The lights started flickering!

"Did you see that?" I asked Billion.

"See what?"

"The lights just flicked on and off!"

"Aw, girl, it's probably just a short. Now finish me off! I did as he asked and noticed the bedroom door was now closed!

"Billion, I think someone is here! That door was open the whole time!" I said, frightened. Billion jumped up and searched the house frantically!

"Do you think it was Bella? She could have come looking for you!

"Hell, no, she would've said something! Get up and get dressed. I want to check out their parent's house!"

Billion angrily stated. Before we went to Mr. and Mrs. Forest's mansion, we stopped by my house to grab the go-cart. They live a few miles on the other side of the lake.

I thought it would be good to take the go-cart through the back gate. That way, we could enjoy the view on the pathway to the mansion.

Before I got in the driver's side of the go-cart. I turned to see someone standing in the window of Landin's master bedroom! It looked like a woman, but I couldn't make out her features!

"What's wrong with you? Your arm has a million goose-bumps on it!"

"I'm fine!" I lied.

"Well, then let's go!" Billion shouted and all I could see was envy in his eyes!

Billion

I tried calling my mother to relish in this lavish life-style that should have been ours in the first place!, but she didn't answer.

I kicked over all the lights aligning the walk-up stairs to Jaylin's parents house. I couldn't wait to destroy this house! When we reached the Hacienda forged iron doors, I felt a cold chill in my bones!

"Are you okay? You look a little pale." English had the nerve to say.

When we opened the door, I expected to see an over-the-top version of those houses you see in the magazines. "What the fuck is this?"

There was a steel wall blocking our entry! So I checked all of the widows receiving the same results!

"Do you wanna say I'm paranoid now, English? These muthafuckers knew we were coming!"

"Or, maybe this is how they secure their home when they are on vacation!"

I've noticed English is very naïve! Fuck it. She is stupid as fuck! The evidence could slap her in the face, and she would say she didn't feel anything!

"I'm out of here! I went next door, and it was the same thing!

I needed to be alone, so I decided to walk back to Bella's house. Right now, I think that was a dumb ass idea because it's dark outside and creepy as hell out here! The fuck was that? Was that an owl? That fucker started cooing which caused me to run to my destination!

"Oh! My! Where have you been? I went down to English's house, and Terry had just arrived! She told me you guys just left the big house! Why would you go with her and not me?" Bella complained.

I tried to move past her to get in the shower to wash English sent off me!

"Why do you smell like a musty fruit, Billion?"

"Damn do you have a dog nose or something? I ate a nectarine from your neighbor's tree!" I laughed to myself.

I showered, brushed my teeth, and swallowed another blue pill! I got some fucking to do tonight, and I need everyone to be satisfied!

"Hey, babe, I think it would be nice to have English and Terry over for drinks. Maybe we can all see what to do next as far as getting those steel walls down."

"I don't see why they need to come here for drinks! We don't need any company."

I didn't expect Bella to agree with having company because she's a jealous attention whore!

"They just want to show a little gratitude for the opportunity I gave them for revenge."

"Yeah, whatever, Terry hasn't even been to Christian and Angel's house! So what does she have to do with revenge?" Bella seethed.

"Stop being a brat! I already invited them, so straighten up!"

"Did you just talk to me like a child Billion?"

"If that's what you think your acting like, then yes!" I said, standing in her face!

I went to the bar cabinet to pick my poison for the night! I pulled out five bottles of Ace of Spades!

I heard Bella suck her teeth as she grabbed the patron!

"What! You don't want this expensive ass champagne? Suit yourself! I'm going to drink up all this shit!"

I sat next to Bella and poured her two double shots!

"Hurry up and drink that shit so you can get in a better mood!"

Bella did what I asked, and soon enough, she started to loosen up!

"Give me some of this fat dick before they come!" Bella started massaging my meat, and right when I was about to pull him out! The doorbell rang!

"We're here!" English announced with another bottle of tequila in her hand! I could feel the heat radiating off Bella's skin!

"What happened to wait until someone answers the door?" Bella directed at English.

"Grrr! Chill out, I come barring gifts!" English held a bag of weed in her other hand!

"Whatever! Can we get on with this toast so yall can go home, and I can hop up and down on my man!" Bella said with an attitude.

"We can all do that later! Let's party!" The look on Bella's face could have killed English dead.

"What the f…."

"Hey, yall?" Terry said from the door, and I froze! Her beauty never ceases to grab my heart! She had on a sheer white bikini with beads cascading down to her sweet honey pot!!

I grabbed the joint English rolled, and lit it up! Then I took two puffs and blew smoke in Bella's face. My goal was to get her so fucked up she'd pass out! This must be some potent shit because Bella is now dancing and feeling on herself!

When I looked around, English and Terry were dancing as well! Terry walked into the hallway and allowed me to taste the sweet chocolate hiding behind her jeweled fabric! "Mmm-mmm! You taste good, love!" It's true! Terry literally tastes like tootsie rolls!

Terry shook uncontrollably from her orgasm. Once she was finished, she ran off to the bathroom! I curiously searched for Bella and spotted her with no clothes on, pleasuring herself on the couch! Loving the sight of her slowly teasing her bud! I became hard as steel!

Before heading Bella's way, Terry reminded me of her juices still on my face! I hurried to brush my teeth and wash my face.

When I reached Bella, she just pulled me down and eased on top of me! She moved back and forth like a snake.

I didn't realize Bella was in a stare-off with Terry and English. Having enough of non-sense, I grabbed the Ace of Spades bottle!

"Open up, baby!"

Bella opened her mouth and drank half the bottle! Bella is a lightweight, so I knew her ass was about to get dizzy!

Next, Terry and English grabbed their own bottles of Ace of Spades. Once Bella came all over me, she passed out right there on the floor in front of the couch. I motioned for Terry to sit back on my face while English wiped me clean and rode me crazy!

I started to get woozy, so I sat up a little with English still riding me! All of a sudden, English jumped up and changed position with Terry! At first, I thought Terry's pussy was so good it made me see things.

The lights started to flicker, and everybody stopped moving! I looked to see where Bella was, and she was still on the floor. I thought for sure our moans would've awakened her! I tried to get Terry off of me, but she was passed out with me still inside her.

I called out to English and got nothing! Suddenly, I saw her trying to get out of the front door, but she slid down to the ground face-first in one instant! I searched for my phone and remembered it had fallen between the couch while recording Bella sucking me off!

Once I found it, I noticed the label on one of the Ace of Spade bottles was hanging off. Slightly scooting up with Terry on my lap, I tore the rest of it off., and It had a question mark on it. I then turned it around, and in a cryptic print of words, read: Love, Thee Elite! Smoke then entered the room, and my body was frozen with fear! I tried to move again but was met with darkness.

Bella: 2 days later

Oh, my head! WHAT THE FUCK! IS THIS BLOOD! The smell was horrid! I was covered in a red sticky liquid with log-stemmed flowers sticking to my skin! After pulling myself up off the floor, I wanted to vomit and strangle my best friend all at the same time!

Terry was on top of Billion, straddling him completely naked. They had flowers and the same sticky red, smelly substance on them as well. English was by the front door face down with what I know now is pigs' blood!

Just then, English eyes popped open and landed on the pig's head, sitting in her direct view.

"AAAAAAAAAAHHHHHHHH!!!!!!" She screamed over and over again! Her screams started to jar Billion out of his sleep, but Terry didn't move!

"Get up, baby!" Billion said to Terry. I thought my ears were playing a cruel joke on me until he repeated it!

"Baby, get up!" he started panicking and slapping her on her face!

"Excuse me? Did you just call her baby?"

"Oh, girl, the jig is up! They have been knowing and fucking each other years before you came along! English said from the door, trying desperately to get the blood off! I searched high and low for something to hit Terry with!

When my eyes landed on Billion's belt still in his jeans. I grabbed it and began to whoop both Terry and Billion's sticky skin! That woke the bitch up! Terry starts to scream and cry!

Pissing me off more and more that Billion hasn't tried to explain what was going on!

I stormed off to the shower, pissed as hell! I could no longer bear the pain! I can't believe I fucked over my husband and child for this muthafucker, who has obviously been playing me this whole time! These muthafuckas are going to get out of my house this instant!

I ran into the room in search of my suitcase when I heard hushed tones!

"Why the fuck did you have to tell her, uh?"

"What the fuck do you mean? You called her baby more than once! You didn't think she caught on to that?"

I needed to know what the fuck was going on, so I finished dressing and grabbed a butcher knife from the kitchen! I went back to the living room, and they weren't there! So I went to the guest bathroom, and they were stepping out of the shower.

"WHO THE FUCK IS GOING TO START EXPLAINING TO ME! WHAT THE FUCK IS GOING ON?" These muthafuckers have the nerve to be in the shower together!

"Oh, no, don't be silent frogs now!" I shouted.

"We have more important matters to deal with, Bella!" Billion yelled!

"Like what asshole! You've been playing me the whole time! You and this bitch!"

"Bitch you had a whole husband that would have done anything for you! And let's not mention the son you've abandoned dead beat ho!" Terry screamed!

I slapped her as hard as I could, and Billion hit me just as hard across the face! I was dumbfounded, to say the least!

"Listen, I needed to get close to you, so I could take back what belongs to my family!" Billion confessed.

"Oh, and I suppose you told him how to get at me, uh! You're a fucking snake, Terry!"

"I'm a snake? You're the one who tried to frame me for killing your grandparents. Talk about evil! Then you had me steal money from your cousin's accounts! Who's the real snake here?"

"So, what now, Billion? You got your piece of the pie! What are your plans for me now!"

"Honestly, you can leave! I don't need you anymore!" Billion shrugged!

"So, you think you're going to live happily ever after? You are a joke, Billion! My husband isn't the type to lay down!"

"EX husband!" he shouted!

"ARE YOU ALL INSANE? We all woke up covered in blood and flowers! I'm sure we didn't do that to each other!" English frantically screamed!

Billion grabbed Terry's hand and pulled her into the living room. I followed, feeling my temperature rising by the minute!

"WHAT THE FUCK!" Billion said, cupping his mouth.

On the bar, there are five full bottles of Ace of Spade champagne! The pig's head is gone, and the blood on the floor has disappeared.

"Someone is in this house! I saw a woman standing in the

window at Landin's place yesterday!" English revealed.

"I think we need to just take the money and run Billion! Let's just go right now!" Terry pleaded!

Billion kissed Terry long and hard on the lips.

"We can't leave yet! Whoever did this did it while we were passed out! flashes of my memories came back at once!

"So were you two fucking while I was passed out on the floor?" Bella shouted. English laughed while shaking her head.

"Bella Bella Bella! I was swirling on his dick, and English was swirling on his tongue!" Terry bragged.

I didn't give her time to walk away! I stabbed Terry in the throat! English screamed and bolted out of the front door in only a bath towel!

Blood sprayed everywhere while Billion held Terry tight and begged her not to die! I didn't give a fuck about his feeling, so I left the room in search of Jaylin's insurance papers. Yes! I have my own money, but I'll be damned if he's not going to give me any of his!

I wasn't expecting the door to the forbidden media room to be unlocked! I was in awe of this room every time Jaylin would allow me inside! Moving further inside the room, I noticed a shiny gold piece of paper that read, play me! I pushed the button and became livid! There Terry bounced up and down on Billion while English rode his face! I watched three more videos of them at his place, engaging in wild sex sessions. Some of them were right after I left his apartment.

I grabbed the butcher knife I pulled out of Terry's neck! My mind was blown, and I was ready to kill Billion! I jumped up in a rage! I was about to walk out of the media room when Billion ran in like a raging bull!

He wrapped his hands around my neck and slammed me on the floor!

"You killed the love of my life, you selfish black bitch! Billion was covered in Terry's blood, with tears running down his face!

"Get off of me, you bastard! I can care less about your bitch!

I tried to run out of the room, but he pulled my hair and swung me into a door I never noticed before! I tried to open the door, and an alarming sound blared through the house! I covered my ears, but that didn't stop Billion from punching me in the face!

"You are the worst kind of bitch! You only care about yourself! You haven't been in your son's room since you 've been here! Just think you were going to run away with me!" Ha! He laughed at me! "I was going ditch your ass and run off with your best friend! He punched me hard!

My sight began to blur, and the sound from the alarm was making my ears bleed! Suddenly I saw the door open, but Billion kept punching me! Quickly, Billion was lifted in the air and thrown through the door!

I couldn't make out who was standing in front of me, but he smelled like Jaylin.

"Jaylin! Baby, is that you? Did you come to save me? I'm so sorry I'll never cheat on you again!" I could feel tears falling from my eyes! "I knew you still loved me, Jaylin!"

"The love I had for you is dead, Bella!" Jaylin's words stabbed me in the heart!

"You can't mean that! He stood up and walked towards the door he came out of. I tried to sit up but was yet again met with darkness.

∞∞∞

A loud voice telling me to get out woke me up! Only when I looked around, no one was there! I leaped up to see that was back in the living room!

The flowers that once covered our naked bodies were now sitting inside a beautiful vase with a note that read:

Since your life is such a bore.

You may freely walk out the door.

Your motto was fun fun fun.

You forgot about your son.

All is lost, and we are done.

Talk about what you've seen, and death will come!

After reading them, the words disappeared, causing me to drop the note and ran full speed to my purse. I didn't even bother with the suitcases I'd stashed in the closet. I drove away with tears in my eyes and vexed because Jaylin had killed me with his words.

All I could think about was Jaylin and the bitch he hired running off into the sunset with my son! For now, I'm going to go! But I'll be back for my son, and no one can stop me!

Chapter 46: Back in the Bunker

Jaylin

You'd think this muthafucka would've given up by now, but his pride won't let him.

"You hit like a bi.." Pop! That was me breaking Billion's nose! Both of his eyes are swollen shut, and this is the tenth time he's called me a bitch, tried to at least.

I don't know if I'm just that good at brawling, or he's that bad at it! Billion won a few fights in an underground brawling room in the background check I did on him! I wanted to test his skills out for myself, so here we are.

Even though I don't have anything left for Bella in my heart! I will never condone a man hitting a woman as Billion had done. That's why I came to her rescue one last time.

"Just tap out, fool! Victorious spoke from the door!" At that moment, Billion hit the floor!

"You probably think you should have left our black asses alone by now, uh? You see, it's all in who you know, not what you heard. Nadia set you up for failure. Or should I say your dad did?" Billion jotted up from the ground, angry with blood dripping from his nose!

"What did you do to my dad and Aunt Nadia?" Billion spat.

"You don't want to know about your mom?" I asked.

"NOOOOOOO! You son of bitch! WHERE IS SHE? I demand to know RIGHT NOW!"

"Well. Just like you, she had a fetish for chocolate!

Linda couldn't leave well enough alone. So we had to show her what it means to not take heed of our words! I'm sure your half-sister warned you before you even got started. So, tell me, Billion, how did all of the plotting and planning work out for you?" Red asked

"Fuck You! Ni..." Plop!

It's been a couple days since we threw Billion down here in one of the torcher chambers. While English was over at my house, participating in the little sessions with Billion and Terry! Raymond's former architect student put up a steel wall behind his front door. Hoping it would deter English from returning.

My brothers and I decided to move to the mansions on the west side of the lake! I don't know what the hell we're going to do with eight bedrooms, but we'll manage!

"How are you all going to get those little rugrats back up-stairs?" Red asked.

Landin stared at Great-Grand Raymond suspiciously, and his eyes shot up to the ceiling.

"ILynn gave them some of those natural nighttime gum-mies," Major said from the door.

"How long is that going to take?" Red sat down impatiently, tapping his foot.

"Since Rose has been giving you some candy. I figured you'd act a lot calmer. You have crackhead traits right now!" Raymond laughed.

"Well, it wasn't enough! She told me to wait until the kids fall asleep and are moved back upstairs!

Look at them over there looking like the children of the corn! ILynn should've given them two of those things!"

"Alright, yall gonna be sitting right next to Bill Cosby's ass!" Landin added with a sly grin aimed at Great-Grand. I just shook my head. Anything dealing with those old men always comes to light.

"I hope you plan on cooking that pig you wasted on them

fools up there! I'm hungry as hell!" Raymond announced!

"Now you know damn well you haven't eaten pork in years! You're going to blow up your intestines messing with that pig!" Red fussed.

I have to admit I'm a little famished. Fucking with Billion, Bella, English, and Terry were draining! The expressions on their faces had us in stitches when they woke up covered in pigs' blood and wildflowers. My Auntie B is nuts! I don't know anyone else who would've come up with that shit!

"Auntie B cut that pig's head off with no remorse! I swear I'll never eat pork again!" Landin complained.

"While yall stomachs are turning, I'm going to be filling mine up with one of those chopped pork slaw sandwiches!" I laughed.

"What are yall doing back there behind that wall?" CJ. Asked.

"Yall need to go ahead and train these inquisitive question-naires! Victorious and I have already been teaching them how to fight!" Raymond bragged under his breath, but I heard him!

Shit! As soon as I get a phone call from the school. I'm going to call his ass call his ass to pick them up! I thought to myself.

"I wish you would!" Raymond said out the side of his

mouth as he walked in front of me! I laughed so hard! I've always believed Great-Grand was a mind reader in real life!

The bedrooms down here are set up like storage units. But inside, the rooms are the size of a studio apartment. As I walked towards the one Vina was in, I heard Sage say.

"I can't wait to get my hands on English and Emery's asses."

"I wish they would've cleared me to take Bella out! I was so close!" Kiley complained.

"Yeah, your restraint game is getting stronger, Sis!" I teased. When my eyes landed on Vina! I saw a twinkle or two in her eyes!

"You ready?" I asked. "Hold on! Now, Vina, did you just hear harp strings when he said that or his regular voice?" ILynn asked, and everyone laughed.

Vina covered her face, and they all squealed!

"See! That shit is real!" ILynn boasted. I took Vina's hand in mine, and she said,

"I wanna stay with you."

Chapter 47: English Rivers

I ran all the way home after running out of Jaylin's house of horror! Reality set in after seeing all the blood cleaned up and all the champagne bottles replenished! Someone was playing games, and I wasn't going to be there for it to continue with me!

When I got here, my guess was in the shower with music blasting! I've been letting her stay here since her mother came up missing! There was no way in hell I was going to go back to Landin's house! I could have sworn someone was watching me get dressed from the doorway of the bathroom.

"Hey, are you okay? You've been sitting there staring off into space for the past three days!" Amber Asked, concerned.

"No! Something is off with Landin and his brothers! I wish I could explain it to you better, but I can't! I just want Landin to hurt as much as my broken heart! fucking Bastard!" I Screamed!

"I hope you're not a weak lovesick puppy like my cousin

Jamie! You see what happened to her, right?"

I just shushed her! I didn't feel like hearing her squeaky voice!

"Your one to talk when your mom is out here spreading it wide for a married man! Hell, you don't even know where she is!"

"I don't care anymore. I'm making my own way out here, and then I'm getting as far away from here as possible!" She seethed.

"Again? You've gotten away from this place several times and keep coming back!" I spat. "You wanna explain that to me, or keep pretending like your not here for a bit of revenge of your own?" I seethed, watching Amber close her yapping mouth.

"Thought so!"

"I'm about to go to the Hats. Are you coming? Sonny's looking for another sub to tame!" Amber confessed.

"Sonny? Amber, if you know what's best for you! You would leave Sonny's ass alone!

I never would have chosen anyone like Amber to be my friend. She's one of those deliberate homewreckers. At first, I thought befriending her would bring me the ultimate satisfaction of watching Jamie squirm.

I know now that Amber is a professional finagler. Which is fine by me if she receives the same ass whoopin Jamie unhinged on my beautiful skin.

Amber waltzed into my living room wearing a sultry chocolate shoulder-length wig! It was perfect for what I have in mind! Resting my head on the back of the couch, I got an email notification that the HOA posted an event:

Please come out and enjoy the Pop Up Splash Pad Obstacle Course Event

Tomorrow Saturday from @noon to 4pm!

Before passing out on my living room floor drunk in sorrow, I'd stepped on my patio to take in some fresh air. I picked up my binoculars and caught a glimpse of movement at Landin's house. This time it was a stranger! A white male in his late 50s standing in the backyard. Soon after, a short black woman and two young female teenagers joined him.

Landin couldn't possibly be moving out, I thought to myself! I put the binoculars down and stormed to my liquor cabinet! Me talking loudly and singing sad love songs is the last thing I remember!

The following day, I got up and ran to the patio doors, where I could see tons of children gathering around the lake!

The scene was fascinating. Zane would've loved this if I wasn't such a shit mother. I can't believe he asked my grandparents to adopt him. Thinking about Zane brings back so many regrets. Had I let Landin be his father figure, We would be married, and I would've been Kelly's mother!

I stopped dead in my tracks from pacing the floor. There Landin was standing behind Sage, holding her tight, sucking on her neck! What the fuck! The last I checked, they were on the outs! Then I saw Kelly! Kelly was so adorable and their pride and joy! Too bad, I'm going to change that!

I put my black Adidas bathing suit on and grabbed one of Zane's floaties out of the garage. I pulled my hair into a high bun, slid my sunglasses on, and headed out towards where Kelly was swimming.

Landin was enjoying himself scarfing down food as I watched Kelly play carelessly on the giant blow-up slide. Adrenaline coursed through my body as I went under the water to grab their precious jewel's feet!

Gotcha!

Chapter 48: Landin Forest

"I'm so glad we taught her how to swim, or else I would be a nervous wreck! Look at all the people!" Sage grabbed my arm to get my attention, but the choice of her bathing suit took the full scope of my sight! I fought with getting what I wanted now or later!

I unsnapped the top of her bathing suit, and my best friends popped out perky and free!

"Landin!" Saged yelped.

"What? They didn't want to be in that tight-ass bikini top anyway! Let me rub on them to make them feel better from being suppressed."

Sage laughed, making them bounce in my face! "Just give me five minutes!"

I kissed my juicy friends, snatched off her bottoms, and dove into my favorite pond! Sage felt so good! Wet and tight! My claim to five minutes turned into an hour in a half.

Since Sage and I made amends! We've been on each other

like a trail of ants marching to a piece of chocolate! Just like right now! Sage bent over in front of me to pick up her discarded bathing suit.

"You must want to stay in here with me all day, uh?"

"No! Now let's go join our family!" She stressed while hopping in the shower!

Why did she do that? I jumped in, and Sage hopped on it again, and that took another thirty minutes!

"OMG! We are going to miss everythinggggggaaa!" Kelly yelled from the door!

It felt eery standing out here, so I took in our surroundings while Kelly ran off to find her cousins.

"Look at the love birds!" Kiley sang, standing in front of us with a scuba diving suit on!

"Why are you dressed like you're about to swim with the sharks!" I laughed!

"Ha, ha, ha! Whatever, knucklehead! This water is cold! You know I have sensitive bones!

"Yo! Is that Victorious on the grill?

Victorious and Great-Grand can throw down on the grill! I made myself a burger, and Sage had the craziest expression on her face!

"Are you really about to eat that double beef cheeseburger while I'm standing here!"

"Sage, I did not take the vegan oath with your ass, okay! I'm about to tear this burger up!"

As I was watching the kids go down the water slide. I noticed a woman abruptly plopped into the water. At the same time, Kiley, who was a little way away, jumped in the water with full scuba diving gear.

The hairs on the back of my neck standing up had me on my feet running towards Kelly, who had just gone underwater! One. Two. Three.

Kelly popped back up! As I entered the water and swam towards my baby girl! I felt several splashes behind me but had no time to look around!

When I got to Kelly, her legs were free, and Kiley was swimming away with the woman I now know to be English! I hope Kiley drowns her ass!

"I kicked that muthafucka in the head!" Kelly bragged. "Isn't that what you told me to do if somebody tries to grab me, Ray Pop!"

I turned around; Great-Grand, Major, Jaylin Christian, and

Ashton, was in the water right behind me!

"That's right, baby, I did!"

"Do you mind explaining how your 96-year-old joints swam over here before me?" Jaylin asked Great-Grand.

"I was already in the water when Landin came rolling through like the Tasmanian devil!"

I spoke Spanish to tell them what I'd seen underwater, and they all swam in that direction.

"Come on, let's go take a rest for a while, Kelly Jelly Belly," I teased while tickling her stomach.

"You know people are going to make fun of me if they hear you say that out loud! Mommy, mommy, I kicked a muthafucka under the water!" Kelly blurted out.

"Kelly! Stop saying muthafucka!" I turned around to Sage, ILynn, Vina and my mother's mouths were hung open!

"Don't act like yall don't know who taught her that word!" I reminded, looking over at Great-grand Raymond, who struggled to get off the floaty he was on. Once again, I spoke in Spanish to tell them what happened.

"Oh! My! God! I thought the guys were chasing you or something! Are you okay, baby? Did they hurt you?"

"No! Mommy, I told you I kicked that muthafu…."

"KELLY!" We all yelled!

"Go with your mom. I'll be right back!" I told Kelly. I need to see what happened!

By the time I drove to the other side of the lake in the go-cart. My cousin BJ was standing there dressed in an EMT uniform!

"Nigga! I can't! When did you become an EMT?" I laughed.

"Since three years ago, fool! Don't knock my hustle! I told yall I'm going to fulfill my dreams before I check out of here!" BJ stated.

BJ led me to the back of the truck to view English's lifeless body and busted skull! I knew she couldn't have survived underwater that long, and not with Kiley pulling her along while she swam to the other side of the lake undetected!

"Where did everybody go?" I asked BJ.

"Major went to erase possible footage from all the nearby cameras; Kiley and Ashton went to inform English's family. And Christian and Jaylin are listening to all the hidden mics around the splash pad."

I can't stop thinking about how this bitch was really going

to drown my baby girl! I felt Sage's arms wrap around my waist.

"Baby, you didn't have to come around here. Everything is going to be okay."

When Sage didn't respond, I turned around to tears running down her face!

"I'm so fucking mad and sad at the same time, Landin! She was going to kill Kelly. English was going to take our child from us because she couldn't have you anymore." Sage cried into my chest.

"English's mother didn't even shed one tear as she shut the door to the ambulance. She tapped the door twice, and BJ drove off! Mrs. Rivers came over and embraced Sage and me.

"I'm so sorry my daughter caused you all so much hell! Had I known what she was planning all those years ago? I would've dealt with her myself." She hugged us again and left.

"Come on, the crowd is starting to dwindle!" I held my wife's hand and led her to the go-cart.

On our way back to the splash pad, I saw a petit woman stand on her tippy toes and kiss Victorious on the lips! I didn't have to ask Sage if she saw it, because just like mine. Her bottom lip shockingly rested on her lap!

"Does it even still work at 96?" Sage inquired.

"Shit! I hope mine still works at that age!"

Chapter 49: Troublemakers End

Eleanor

"I know you know how to work one of those tractors over there, Rose. Weren't you raised on a farm?" Celia asked.

"What the hell do I look like sitting on a tractor all day? My dad and uncles did all that shit!" Rose responded.

"Oh, hush up, gals. I know how to use one! I do have a profound garden in my backyard!" I reassured.

"Oh, well, excuse me, black Martha Stewart! Rose said with her hand resting on her chest!.

I pulled myself to the seat of the tractor and got to work on digging the new area of our wildflowers. Driving this thing is like riding a bike, and once you learn how you'll never forget.

I was in awe of the assorted colors and different kinds of graceful flowers! Splendid in their own right, I'm sure without our unique blends of horror. They would flourish beautifully, but a little extra help never hurt anything.

"Grandmother, what are you doing up there on that big ass

tractor! We're ready to get this party started," ILynn yelled up to me. These youngsters today are so impatient!

"Hop up here so I can school you on some things! It takes preparation and skill to do what we do!

"Oh! Wow! This is outstanding! Looking at it from up here makes me appreciate it more! I'm not saying you wouldn't adore the view of driving or walking by. But up here, they are captivating!" ILynn assessed.

We just sat there in silence , star gazing at the beautiful scene!

"Uh! Yall wanna get down here so we can get out of this hot ass sun? Shit! The mosquitoes love my sweet perfume! Reminds me of Red's ass always on me! Rose added while smacking her own neck.

"Did you just call me a mosquito?" Red asked while again popping up out of nowhere.

"Damn, Red do you want to kill me? I mean, my heart drops every time you do that!"

"You probably shouldn't be talking about me like that then!"

"Where's Bobbye?" I frantically asked. I'd hope she wasn't in the barn plucking out their eyeballs because I wanted them to see everything we had prepared for them.

Auntie B

"**I**'m right here!"

I grabbed Nadia by her hair as she tried to drop her weight to the ground! Her inability to walk doesn't phase me, though.

"Why don't you just kill me already! she shouted

Nadia's hair is a matted mess and smells like the shit she's been rolling in!

"UGH! She stinks!" Dom griped, holding his nose.

"You didn't say any of that when you were fucking her in the garage now, were you?"

"Well, she didn't stink... Let me shut up!" Dom mumbled under his breath.

"Yeah. Nigga you act like my sister isn't unstable with those pluckers she calls fingernails! Now, let's go get the others," Red called out.

"OHHHH! Help me, Dom! Please don't let her kill me! I

know you still want me, baby! We can even run off together! I can see it in your eyes. You want me. I know it! She can't satisfy you like I can! Come on, show me that big di...." PLUCK!

"AAAAAAA!!! AAAAAAAA! AAAAAAAAA! MY EYE! OH! MY! GOD! MY EYE!!!!!!!!!! AAAAAAAA!"

I couldn't take it anymore. Nadia's disrespect, even in her current situation, was mind-boggling! I mean, she saw what I did to Dom's eye! I don't know why she thought she'd get a pass.

"AUNT NADIA! OH! MY! GOD! WHAT DID YOU DO TO HER! LET ME GO! AAAAAAAHHHHH!" Billion hollered.

Red hit him over the head.

"She snatched my eye out!" Nadia cried loudly!

"SOMEBODY HELP ME! I DON'T HAVE ANYTHING TO DO WITH THIS!" Tyra spat!

"So, you didn't give Billion weapons to use against us, or better yet, tamper with our gun order? Don't look so surprised. We see and know everything." Major announced.

"Besides, do you want to rot in prison for the rest of your life, sloppy girl? I showed Tyra footage of her face being plastered all over the news.

"You're a wanted woman for killing your parents in cold

blood!" I then showed her footage of her killing her parents after they confronted her about the side deals she'd been cutting.

"The way I see it is, this will be your karma for killing such fine people! Your parents were one of a kind allies, and you fucking ruined it!"

Now that the whole gang is here, I went to grab the last troublemaker.

"Come on, Hershey booty! I was surprised Emery didn't put up a fuss! I admired how she took ownership of trying to fuck up my great-nephew's marriage.

Ella dug four new rows on the other end of the wildflowers. But first, I wanna have a little fun! I've instructed everyone to put on their beekeeper suits!

"I know you all have seen Fear Factor. Well, today, you four will feel the sting you so desperately inflicted on this family."

While Emery, Billion, Nadia, and Tyra racked their brains. Dom rolled out a rectangular glass showcase box! Perfect for four people.

"I'm not getting in there! What is this, Dom! Help me, baby, please! You don't really want to do this." Nadia cried with a deflated ass cheek." I pushed her in the box first!

"You're going to have to shoot me!" Billon yelled. BLOC! Jaylin shot Billion in the foot and threw him in the box. Sage and ILynn tossed Emery and Trya in last.

In this experiment, I will need pineapple juice and some sugar, lots of it!

ILynn did the honors of pouring the pineapple juice and sugar on the troublemakers from the top of the box.

"You come up with the cruelest punishments," Red mentioned. Dom brought out the bees, and the troublemakers went fucking nuts!

It was so funny to watch them slipping over one another and trying to hold themselves up against the glass.

"OOHH, these bees are about to sting yall asses up!" Rose stressed, wearing an oversized bee suit.

I've never seen the running man quite like this before! Billion looked like he caught the spirit! I let the bees sting for about three minutes, then fumigated them so we could move to the next phase of torture!

"Dom, can you hand me the salt, please?" Dom handed me the salt, and I emptied the full containers on their opened wounds! The screams were so loud; my ears rang!

"Okay, okay! Now for the Grand Finale!" I led them to their

own personal wood chipper!

Dom already had the machines positioned in all four rows! Jaylin stood behind Billion, I stood behind Nadia, ILynn stood behind Tyra, and Sage stood behind Emery.

"I would like to tell you all a little story and sing you a little song!" Victorious said from behind us.

Victorious's story always brings me to tears.

"I didn't have anything to do with this family war! I don't even know any of you like that! Emery's submissive behavior suddenly found her voice!

"No, but you were happy to see my pain, and for that, you gotta go!"

Sage pushed Emery in the shredder! And we all followed her lead! CLUNK, CHUCK, CLACK, CRACK, BOOSH! BOOSH! BOOSH! BOOSH! Their heads burst like watermelons! "UGH! BLUA! BLUA!" ILynn threatened. "ILynn, You better not! That throw-up is going to be in that suit with your ass!" Major warned.

Chapter 50: Victorious, Raymond and Miss hot to trot

These young girls really think all old men are desperate and eager to give their AARP benefits to their asses! Ha! Jokes on them. I just want the weed! Janine and her daughters have the best weed in the city! And as long I feel like I'm 50 years young, I'm going to be miss Janine's sponsor.

Does my Johnson still work? I'm sure it does. The last time I used it, that muthafucka almost caused a heart attack! So, now I just smoke my weed, eat, and go to sleep! I'm too damn old to be trying to tame some coochie! However, This new weed has my Johnson soluting to the roof! Sometimes involuntarily!

"Let's go dancing, Victorious!" Janine said from the other room.

"You know this nigga is not going to go dancing with your hot to trot ass! Out here giving it up to the whole neighborhood!" Raymond remarked, coming through the front door!

"It was just a thought," Janine sassed.

"And as far as me giving it up! Yall won't give me any, so what am I supposed to do?"

"What the hell do we look like risking our lives to make your toes curl for a few minutes! And why would anybody want some 96-year-old dick!" Raymond questioned.

"Ugh! What are yall in here talking about?" Janine's 26-year-old Manish daughter, Candy, asked.

I couldn't stop laughing! You would think those two were married! Janine is 55 years old out here, still trying to get a baller! I get It, though. Janine's body is insane. She has a country cornbread-fed booty! Beautiful brown blemish-free skin and a sexy smile. Her daughters aren't far behind in the looks department.

She has natural curly shoulder-length hair but likes to wear those $3000 weaves that flow past her waist.

"Are you done with our batch of goodies, yet I think I'm being followed by one of my greats! Nosy fuckers!" Raymond complained.

"Man! I'm out of here! I told Janine that little display of affection was going to cause trouble. If Angel and ILynn ever find out about this! It's a wrap!"

Knock! Knock! "Aww, hell, you led them, jokers, right to us! I need you to start wearing your glasses, Raymond! Your senses are impeccable, but your eyesight sucks!"

I got two feet from the back door when Major walked right through it! "Where do you think you going, old man?"

"Yeah, yall are busted! Now come on and get your things. Playtime is over for you as well!" Landin had the nerve to say to Raymond. Who is now standing there with his mouth open?

"I'm sorry, what are you going to do with that equipment?" Janine asked Major.

"Hand me those packages you were about to hand over to my Greats." Major's cold, impassive tone made Janine move quickly.

"What is this, Victorious? You don't trust us!" Janine perked up!

"He does, but we don't," is all she's getting out of Major.

"Ooooh, why yall didn't tell me it was some sexy ass men down here! Hi, my name is Sugar, and you are?"

"Wondering if your momma had cavities giving yall sugar bug names! What's your middle name? Bear?" Landin quizzed.

"As a matter of fact, it is!" Sugar giddily replied.

"THAT'S IT! Nigga hurry up so we can get the hell out of here!" Landin demanded at Major's back!

"Alright, yall good to go! I just needed to check and see if this shit was safe and not laced with something. Yall out here getting around better than the average 45-year-old!

"Whatever, let's go yall just embarrassed our old asses like we're not decades older!" I feel like a teenage boy getting caught with my pants down!

"Wait! Don't you want to know how sweet I am? Sugar desperately called out to Landin. "I know you saw the wedding rings on both those men's fingers, Sugar!" Candy informed.

"What was the point of all that back there?" I asked Major and Landin.

"The point was for me to get the ingredients so yall can cut ties with miss-hot to trot! Janine is not only selling weed; she and her plaque-mouthed daughters are selling hot pussy pies also!" Landin revealed.

I just shook my head and told Raymond to meet me at our other spot. We may be 96 years old, but we still find fun things to do.

Chapter 51: Vina

I just received a massive check from my ex's lawyers. But not without a threat to go with it. Pete just won't leave well enough alone when it comes to me! I mean, what else does he expect from me. I was so humiliated by his insecurities. Like right now.

Pete: I'm going to leave you alone for now, but don't get comfortable. I'll be back soon!

I thought about showing Jaylin the text but changed my mind. I don't want to dampen my mood of having him here in my home. I'll just take what little peace I can get from that psychopath. I hope he bumps his head or drives off a cliff in the process.

Jaylin surprised me this morning by joining me on my morning run! I'd mentioned running along the beach every morning before work. It gives me time to think about my life and give praise to the Lord above. This morning was different, though, and I prayed for Jaylin to find peace and happiness.

The things I've learned about his and Bella's relationship are stressful, to say the least. If I had access to this sexy ass man every day, I would be hitting all my high notes! Here I go again with my thoughts. I gathered the things I needed for work and headed for my shower.

"OH! You scared me!" I jumped at the sight of him.

Jaylin is standing in the doorway of my room with only a towel wrapped around his waist! I can't even look away from his massive bulge! Oh, my goodness, it makes me want to sing!

"I would love to hear you sing." Jaylin spook from the door.

Wait, did I say that shit out loud? "Uh, did; do you need something?" I stuttered.

"Yes, as a matter of fact, I need some lotion."

I could have sworn I stocked the guest bathroom with tons of lotion. "Did you check under the sink?" I asked In a very nervous tone. He turned to go check, and I hauled ass to the shower!

As I lathered my mango body soap over my body. My temperature rose with the thought of Jaylin kissing me all over my body! I'm no slouch when it comes to sex. Thus the reason my ex went crazy! As for me, I haven't been satisfied in years!

I stood under the shower cotemplating on pleasing myself.

Jaylin got me so hot and bothered that a cold shower would be useless. After I stepped out of the shower, I realized my clothes were still lying on the bed.

Not fully dry, I slipped on my robe and opened the bathroom door. I wish I could say that the cold air was the sole reason for my hardened nipples poking out of my robe. But, there Jaylin was sitting in the on the chair in the corner of my room.

"The lotion I need isn't under the sink," Jaylin announced.

I grabbed the lotion off of my bathroom counter and handed it to him. Jaylin's fingertips brushed up against my melting skin. Don't ask me why I didn't move from my spot. And don't ask me why I didn't close my robe, exposing both of my fully erect nipples.

When I tried to close my robe, he shook his head no. Jaylin's hypnotic hazel eyes darkened with passion as he slid my robe off with both his index fingers!

"Mmmmm!" I didn't mean to moan out, but his simple touch struck my vocal chord. And when he kissed me, sensational jolts of electricity coursed through my music box!

I didn't know how bold and eager I was until I untucked his towel! Jaylin was blessed in the department below, so I had to brace myself! I sat on the edge of my bed and welcomed his gentle yet demanding touch! Jaylin kissed me from head to toe and then pierced my soul as a vampire would his prey.

"Sssssss! There is the lotion I needed," he whispered in my ear!

My lotion provided him hydration as he slow danced inside my creamy center.

"You feel so good; I wanna watch you take all of me, Vina. Jaylin moved me on top of him as he watched me slowly meltdown his long thick magic wand! I already knew once he reached my spot. I was never letting go! Dickmatized? Yes.

Chapter 52: JLynn Forest: Black Friday

"I don't know why the hell I agreed to come out to this mall today! And with the kids at that! We could have sat in front of the computer and pushed a button!" Angel complained.

"Where's the fun in that? Besides, the kids wanted to shop for the family."

MayLynn has been bugging me to take her to the mall. She wants to buy everyone Christmas gifts. Once MayLynn shared her idea, the other kids followed, and it became a group thing.

Once again, we caught a break on Christmas shopping for our kids. Because Auntie B bought and wrapped their presents and put them under our Christmas trees, Spoiled brats!

"Mommy, look at that watch but don't look too long! It will blind you. It's so shiny and blingy! I think Red Pop would love it!"

"OOOhhhh! Weeee, this watch is sweet! Kyle countered.

"I wonder if they have one in my size!" Chris added.

"Uh, we are here to shop for others, not ourselves!" Angel reminded.

After we headed inside the store to get coser view, the kids went wild.

"Oh! Wow, Aunt ILynn, these earrings will look lovely on Nanna Rose!" Ashley sang!

"I think your right, Ashley, but don't tell anyone I'm about to get them for myself as well!" We chuckled.

"I'm getting this necklace for nanna Celia," Kelly boasted and already talking to a sales clerk. The clerk took out the diamond-encrusted piece and placed it on the counter!

"What do yall think? Kelly asked. She's going to love it! We all responded.

I picked out a bracelet for my grandmother and a few cuff links for Victor Sr. while choaching myself not to look at the necklaces.

"Okay, your total comes to $35,874. I handed the clerk my black card and heard a few whispers. I was just about to ask where Junior was when he waltzed past me with three jewelry bags.

"Junior, I told you I would pay for everything, and what clerk checked you out and didn't ask questions?"

"Oh, that was Johnathan apparently; he knows little Junior because he and his dad came in here the other day! I remember because I had to tell my co-worker to stop flirting with his dad!" The clerk shook her head!

I'm still stuck on Junior purchasing expensive items without a parent! "Hey, Junior baby, you can't just go off and make big purchases by yourself. There are bad people out here just looking for the opportunity to snatch something from you!"

"I got this, Auntie! I know just what to do!" I shot my eyes over at the group of guys standing there with their tongues hanging out!

"Okay, I think we should go now. We've attracted some unwanted attention." I told Angel before alerting our security detail to grab our bags and take them to the house. I didn't want to risk it being stolen.

Afterward, we headed out to the parking lot with the kids in front of us. Unfortunately, I saw those same guys walkout as well. But this time, my senses went up! Those are the guys

Serta was with at the salon.

"Well, don't you look cute! I have that same sweater dress and boots." I heard Serta say from behind me.

I chose my words carefully because I didn't want her to misunderstand.

"The fuck you want, Seta?"

"Aw! don't be like that. I only wanted to introduce you to my cousins because they moved here from Alabama and need someone to decorate their house."

"Yeah, I want you to decorate my face with your legs wrapped around it!" One of the guys mumbled while grabbing his package. That ass is fat as fuck! Let me touch it!

"You look like one of those undercover freaky bitches!" The other guy stated while flicking his tongue.

"Uh, she is definitely a freaky bitch if Major married her over me. Yall should get a taste while I record a little video for my man to see. Maybe he'll give me some more of that stupendous dick!

While these nasty muthafuckers surrounded me. Serta stepped back and took out her phone! Just as I went to grab my butterfly knife out of my hair! All three guys, including Serta, hit the ground like dominos! Now sit back because I'm about to describe what happened in slow motion!

Angel and the kids walked a little way before they noticed I wasn't right behind them. But that didn't stop the Black-eyed Taekwondo kids from putting on a show! MayLynn jumped off the trunk of a car and landed on guy one's back, Snatching his eye out the socket!

Kyle kicked guy two in the nuts causing him to bend over in pain. Kyle didn't stop there, though! This little Ninja turtle snatched the guy's tongue right out of his mouth and said,

"Watch your muthafuckin language when speaking to a lady!"

Then for the grand finale! Junior, who I had no idea, harbored the darkness! Walked up to Serta and guy three in slow motion like a Transformer with sparks of fire falling to the ground! I kid you fuckin not! Junior's arms extended out like the rubber band man smashing both of their noses in like a pancake.

Even though our second security was standing there, shocked and discombobulated! The only word my brain registered at that moment was RUN!

We all sat in silence on the way home. When I looked in the rearview mirror. The kids were sleeping like they didn't just mortal combat those fools back there.

Angel hasn't said a word, and that is definitely unusual. "I want to be upset about them being trained so early. But after seeing what happened tonight! I'm grateful!

"They kicked the shit out of those farmhouse assholes! Shit, you better fuckin sleep with your bedroom door locked! Did you see MayLynn fly through the air like one of those black-eyed Power Puff Girls?" Angel laughed, finally finding her voice.

Chapter 53: Jaylin Forest and his suspicions

"**M**an, look at you! You're happy; happy! I haven't seen your smile reach your eyes over a woman in years!" Landin admitted and patted himself on the back!

"I know Vina is unlike any other. Besides her being perfect, She's excellent with Junior!"

"You mean the Optimus Prime?" Landin corrected.

I watched the video countless times with the same re-action! He moved just like Major!

"What's up? Why did you call me over at this time of night?" Major complained, walking through the door. "Aww, hell, this nigga grouchy, you better make this quick!" Landin joked and laughed.

I was just about to speak when our grandfather Red, nanna Rose, Victor Sr., and Ella moseyed in the door!

"Oh! This must be bad if you called them here at this hour. Major remarked.

A few months ago, the greats said something that got my attention. So instead of telling you. I'll show you! I got up and walked towards the entryway of my bedroom closet. In my old house house, the tunnels' entrance, was in my linen closet, which was a little cramped.

"You got some taste, young blood!" Red admired walking through my new house. As soon as I pulled the latch, I was hit with questions.

"Why are we going in the tunnel? I'm too cute to get spider webs in my hair!" Nanna Rose complained,

"When we get down here, do not overreact too quickly!" I advised.

The tunnels are wide enough to drive the go-carts. But there are only two entryways to get them in and out. So, I made sure to get one of the go-carts to my end of the tunnel so we wouldn't have to walk the mile to our destination.

"I haven't been down here in years! Clearly, somebody else has because it's clean as a whistle." Red gathered.

I stopped short of our destination and told them to listen. Screeching, howling, whispering, wailing, and whimpering moans could be heard throughout the tunnel!

All of their lightbulbs must have come on at the same time. Because when I turned around, they'd covered their mouths. But not for long, though.

"Those old head buzzards are the ones who have been hunting the Gruffs house!" Red muttered.

"Shh! Do you hear that? Victorious asked Raymond.

"Hear what, fool? Did you put your hearing aide in your ear?" Raymond asked Victorious.

"I don't have a hearing aide!"

"Aww, shit! Victorious, I went with you to go pick it up last week! They should've checked your memory too!

I couldn't stop nanna Rose if I wanted to! She leaped out of the go-cart so fast. 5 4 3 2 1!

"VICTORIOUS BELL CROSS and RAYMOND WAYNE FOREST! YOU OUGHT TO BE ASHAMED OF YOURSELVES! DOWN HERE TERRORIZING INNOCENT PEOPLE!

Yall had people moving out of that house, believing it was haunted!"

"Tell him, Rose! Now let's go pack him up for the living

assistant program down the street!" Red taunted while doing a little shuffle!

"I wish you would send me to that place! I'll haunt your ass till I die! And after too! Fuck wit me!" Raymond shouted.

"I don't know what you're smiling about, Victorious, you're going to go with him! Out here driving my car around like a ventage pimp and sponsoring the neighborhood thot!" Victor Sr. added

I could see it before it happened! Victorious reeved up the tricked-out go-cart and sped off like hellfire! He took off so fast; Great-grand Raymond's dentures flew out of his mouth! The expression on his face took us all out! Just imagine an old man about to cuss you out with no teeth!

"Yall know they're about to catch a flight to one of the islands," Landin informed.

Victorious and Raymond run off to one of the fully-staffed islands we own when they get tired of us telling them what to do!

"We'll let them go for now." Victor Sr. agreed.

Chapter 54: Jamie Winters (White)

"How long are you going to ignore me, Sonny? I said I was sorry it was an accident! Last weekend Sonny and I invited a few of our friends from the Dungeon to go out with us! I suggested the club Layeres because it's the hottest club in the city.

Sonny didn't think I was aware of his past relationship with one of the ladies we invited. I watched them closely because I refused to become a victim like Tammy. Sonny fucked me right under her nose for months, and I'll be damned if he does me the same.

Tammy's death didn't slow us down, though. Sonny refused to hide our relationship any longer! Tammy's father was furious, but what could he do! Tammy changed her will; therefore, Sonny received all of her money.

The bartender came around to take our drinks, but some

of the ladies went to the restroom. I needed to freshen up, so I headed in that direction.

"Do you think she knows you're still subbing for him!"

"I just had a session with him before we came here! And get this, he was already having a session with someone! I just invited myself to the party!" I heard the ladies say while I hid behind the door.

I had a one-track mind as the click of my heels led me to Sonny. I was going to slap the shit out of him and be done! Only my steps were compelled. Major was caressing his beloved wife's plump ass moving to the song Slow motion. By Trey Songs.

I fell into a trance! It was as if my feet were plugged into a high voltage of electric currents. Flashes of Major holding my body close to his kickstarted a well-known inferno down below!

As I lost all sense and control. I was no longer mad at Sonny; in fact, I needed him to put this volcano out! I grabbed Sonny and led him to a hall closet I'd passed on the way to the restroom. Sonny is fully aware of my addiction and sometimes plays on it from time to time.

The closet was small, but I didn't care! I jumped on Sonny

and rode him like a bull! I came five times within minutes with Major's name full on my lips! I didn't even know what I'd done wrong until a few days ago!

"You know since you like saying Major's name while we're fucking and in your sleep! You should probably go be with him." Sonny shouted while trying to walk out of the door, but I stopped him.

"It's funny how you're playing the victim when you've been fucking the bitch we invited to the club last week!"

"Yet instead of you confronting me about it. You wanted to fuck my brains out because you saw Major. So, I'm going to show you how that shit made me feel in the worst way, Jamie!" Sonny countered as he pushed past me and slammed the door!

I popped a bottle of wine and sat there thinking about why I couldn't shake the thought of Major hammering into my soul! I sat and waited on Sonny to come back home for hours. Then an idea popped in my head! Sonny loves when I submit spontaneously.

I grabbed the handcuffs and cuffed myself to the bed! because the effects of the wine had me feeling way past right! I hadn't realized I'd fallen asleep util i heard a little commotion!

"Ohhhh, Oooh Oooh, right there, Sonny! Yes! Yes! Yes!

Baby! You're going to make me cum so hard!" I heard a familiar voice say!

"You are so wet!" I heard Sonny say.

As I opened my eyes, I began to go into a rage! There, my cousin, Amber, was fucking my man at the end of our bed! Sonny lifted Amber's leg up to have a clear view of his thick, elongated member moving in and out of her leaking twat. My screams and pleas made him fuck her harder, and she loved every minute of it!

He picked her up and put her legs over his forearms. Sonny then turns to face me, giving me a full view of Amber's ass spread wide. He then smiled at me as he hammered into her over and over.

"Fuck! Fuck! Fuck!" Amber squealed as her juices coated Sunny's steel tool!

Sonny then hiked her up on the dresser, where he again held her legs open as he feasted on her peach as if it was the best pie known to man! I was numb! My heart shattered into a million pieces as I realized how Carmen, Tasha, and Tammy felt!

I never felt remorse before now! It made me feel guilty for my nonchalant standards. I yanked and pulled as hard as I could until I heard a crack in the wood my cuffs were locked on.

I quickly uncuffed myself while Sonny was flicking Amber's clit at a fast pace. That bitch was in awe, whimpering with her head hanging back! I put my clothes back on and chucked the cuffs right at Amber's face, hitting her in the mouth! She screamed in agony as blood poured from her mouth.

I grabbed the piece of wood off the floor, and was just about to beat Sonny. When the door flew open! There was a very tall man standing in the doorway with a gun pointing right at Sonny's head!

"Is this the type of shit you were doing to my daughter? Is this why she had a heart attack? You fucking bastard! You killed her, didn't you? And who are these bitches? Is this the whore you had living with you and my daughter?" Tammy's father venomously yelled, pointing at Amber.

Amber tried to run, but the gun went off, sending several shots throughout the room! Blood ran down my chest as I registered being shot in the neck! The force of the bullet knocked me back on the bed as I watched Tammy's dad unload his clip inside Amber and Sonny!

Meanwhile, I was fading away into darkness when I saw my

mother with a gun of her own, aiming it at the gunmen! BLOC, a single shot, blew his head off!

Suddenly I heard her screams and felt her tears on my face.

"I was coming to take you home and get you more help! I didn't want to give up on you just yet!" My mother cried.

At that moment, all I wanted to do was go home with my mother! The love I felt from her touch made me happy and sad as I felt my life slip away. As I took my last breath, I told my mother, "Thank you!"

Chapter 55: The Island for Christmas

Landin & Sage

"Come on, Sage, you're going to make us late getting to the plane!" I'm standing outside the Chocolate Cup Coffee Shop, waiting for slowpoke Sage in her Naomi Cambell walk stilettos to pick up the pace.

I wanted to see if we could catch Miss Alice because we missed her the last few times.

"Hold your horses. I'm trying to break my new heels in!" She snapped. If she only knew what she looked like clicking up here in slow motion! I ought to record her looking like a baby horse trying to walk!

We walked in, and as usual, the coffee shop was packed. Sage took a seat in our favorite area.

"What do you want, babe?" I asked.

"Uhm, just get me a hot chocolate." She replied without

looking up. I just stood there and stared at my baby pact trappin ass wife! Sage is a Cappuccino queen; hell, she turned me on to it!

I just shook my head because we were all conned by our women on Thanksgiving five years ago. Then on Christmas Eve, our wives told us we would become fathers! We were so happy and overjoyed we didn't see the sly grins on their pretty little faces. Like right now, Sage is desperately trying not to show hers.

Hi, I need two Cappuccinos and one hot chocolate, and can you have Miss Alice bring them to us, please?"

"Miss Alice?" the cashier asked with a confused look on her face.

"Yes, the lady in that picture behind you!" I huffed, getting frustrated.

"Uhm, sir, my mother passed away ten years ago."

I stood there for a long ass time knowing damn well.

"So, if she died ten years ago, that means the person who's been bringing me my drinks is a...."

"It's okay, sir; I see her from time to time also!"

I peeled off $300 bills and put them in the young lady's tip jar.

"SAGE!" I yelled, earning everyone's attention.

I rushed to our section, and Sage wasn't there! I turned to the glass doors and gasped. There Miss Alice was handing an Emerald green box to Sage! I high-stepped like a marching band, grabbed Sage's hand, and galloped the hell out of the coffee shop.

"Bye, and thank you! Miss Alice! Let's go, Sage!"

"OH! MY GOD! WHAT HAS GOTTEN INTO YOU!" That was so rude! I was saying thank you! Why did you do that?" Sage handed me the gift Miss Alice gave her, and it read Guardian Angel.

"Babe!" I said, out of breath "When I went up to the counter to request Miss Alice, her daughter said she'd passed away ten years ago!"

"So, the person I was just talking to was…."

"A muthafuckin GHOST!"

Kiley & Ashton

I think I drank too much eggnog when I once again agreed to join the baby pact! I honestly didn't think I would get pregnant so soon after ditching my birth control! Obviously, all sense of common sense was nowhere to be found. Don't get me wrong, I love the twins! It just ripped my lady parts to shreds giving birth to those lovable big-headed babies!

I haven't said a word since I found out this morning! But Ashton can read energies almost better than me.

"Why are you just sitting there? We have to get to the plane! I'm not getting cussed out by your mom this time." Ashton fussed.

"I'm ready! Let's go, geez! Let's stop at Dunkin donuts. I'm starving!"

"Hold up! Didn't you just eat?"

Shit! "Yeah, I wanna grab some donuts for the kids! You

know my mom has indeed turned into health gurus! She loves to make those blueberry banana oat Acai bowls for the kids. And they pretend to love them." I said, watching Ashton cover his mouth with his fist.

"Man, come here with your pregnant ass!" Ashton picked me up and smashed his lips into mine!

"I love the hell out of you, and I'm happy as hell you're giving me another set of twins!"

See what I mean! Either he's that good, or I gave myself away. What was I thinking? I wasn't, that's what!

Christian & Angel

"Baby, did you print out the food list?" Angel asked me a mile away from the plane.

"If I forgot the list, it would be too late to get it, right?"

"What crawled up your ass, Christian?

You've been snapping at me for weeks now!" I shook my head at Angel because she knows damn well why I'm snappy.

For the past few weeks, I've experienced Angel's morning sickness. Same as I had done with Chris., I should've known what was up when she insisted on sitting on my dick. After telling her I was sleepy! I'd eaten so much food on Thanksgiving. Sleep was all I wanted to do!

Christmas is my favorite time of year. Especially drinking the spiked eggnog and sweet potato pie! Now I can't even eat that shit because the thought of it has my stomach turning. Fuck! I know I sound like a crybaby, but fuck it!

"Well, did you bring the list or not?" Angel asked AGAIN! I just handed the list to her, hoping she would be quiet! Her yapping amplified my migraine!

"Damn! You couldn't just say, yes Jeez, it's like pulling teeth with you lately!"

"ANGEL, if I didn't love you to death or if you weren't possibly carrying my twins. I would take your seatbelt off, mash the fuck out of this break, and watch you fly through the muthafuckin windshield!" I said, meaning every word I just spat.

"DAMN!" Angel replied. Clutching her pearls, she leaned back in her chair. But not for long!

"Do you think I ought to make the sweet potato cheesecakes tonight or in the morning?"

"You mean the Cali Love Pies you've been passing off as your own for years?" I revealed as Angel damn near flatlined. But recovered quickly.

"Do I need to pop my titty in your mouth or something? Maybe, yo ass will stop being so grumpy!" Angel mumbled under her breath.

"I don't know if I was supposed to hear that or not, but I did! And I would pop those Hershey kisses right in my mouth if

I weren't having your morning sickness," I announced.

"Shit!" Angel said, finally realizing. All of her secrets are out.

JLynn & Major

"**W**hat's wrong with yall?" I asked Sage and Landin. They both looked like they saw a ghost as they boarded the plane! Sage and Landin were unusually quiet the whole entire plane ride!

"I'll tell you later," Sage uttered, as Landin started shaking his head from side to side!

"Don't tell anybody that shit! They might send our asses to one of those asylums." Landin countered.

I gotta know now! I'll just wait until later.

I can't even begin to tell you how magnificent this Island is! Not to mention the beach house! It has 15 bedrooms and three pools that run off into the ocean! The crystal clear turquoise water matches my maxi dress, and the white sand is the same color as my toenails.

As I stood on the deck of our bungalow, I let my hair down so the wind could dance through my tresses.

"I'll never get tired of looking at you, baby." Good chills ran up my spine at the sound of Major's deep voice! Even now, the butterflies in my stomach swarm at the sight of him!

Major led me back inside as everyone got ready to bombard the Great-Grands private headquarters! No, they don't know we're here, and personally, I can't wait to see the look on their faces.

Major picked me up and sat me on top of the kitchen counter! He then bent down and kissed my stomach!

I froze because I hadn't told him I was expecting yet!

"How did you know?

"The way you took me on Thanksgiving!

But, You see, Agua Azul, I know your body inside and out. You were already carrying my seed! So you will have to tell your little mommy pact trappers you're going to deliver a month early!

Now come on, everyone is ready, and you have the key to their room in your purse."

"Wait, are Jaylin and Vina flying out today or tomorrow?" I asked because they didn't make it to the plane.

"No, his whipped ass is spending Christmas with Vina and

her family."

"Oh, Vina is about to be the sister-in-law for real, for real!" We both laughed!

"I can't wait to surprise Ray Pop and Three G Victorious." MayLynn raved. I told everyone to be quiet before I opened the door! This is where Major and I ran off to for the weekend a couple months ago!

As soon as I opened the door, I shut it! All the prayers in the world couldn't make me unsee what I just saw! I'm trying hard not to puke!

"What's wrong, baby? Why did you shut the door?" Major fret concerned.

"Let's just say. It still works! The shock and horror on everyone's faces gave way back to our rooms like grounded teenagers!

The Great- Grands had two Island thots hopping up and down on their ancient artifacts! Merry Christmas!

" Rose, we gotta get some of that weed!"

"Shut up, Red!"

Chapter 56: Bella: A Year Later

I've been all over the world, changing my appearance. My first stop was Africa because I wanted to get my eyes permanently changed to green! It took three months to clear up, but it was well worth the wait! The attention keeps me gassed up like a thousand fuel pumps!

The next stop was my nose; it was long and skinny, and I hated it! I gave the doctor a picture of ILynn's nose because she had a perfect one. I also took a page out of Emery's book and got my skin lightened.

No, I wasn't ashamed of my skin color. I just wanted to be able to walk around freely. I'm not sure why I haven't seen my face plastered all over the news for killing my Grandparents. However, I wouldn't dare be as careless to think my cousins aren't after me for it. Ha! Good luck finding me now!

I could have raised the phoenix sun when I saw my son walk down the aisle as a ring barrier to Jaylin and Vina's wedding! How dare he marry his quote-on-quote assistant! Vina was fucking beautiful, and Jaylin looked happier than he ever was with me! I cried ugly tears when he sank his lips into hers.

There wasn't a dry eye in the building as he recited his vows. Thinking back on our wedding, we just repeated what the pastor said. There were no heartwarming words whatsoever! I didn't care. All I cared about was how he looked as if he couldn't wait to tear my dress off.

I blended in with the crowd as best as possible, and I made sure not to get too close to any of Jaylin's family. Sitting on the bride's side was a bit risky as well. People kept asking me who I was. Probably because of the tears, but those couldn't be helped.

Junior looked at Vina like his birth mother, which made me want to snatch his little ass up and shake him to death. I wondered if junior missed me, so I sent him the second edition of books I used to read to him before bed.

Of course, I used a P.O box. And wouldn't you know! This little bastard not only sent them back, but left me a message as well:

I could never feel your heartbeat when you hugged me. Your kisses were cold, and your words were meaningless. Now that you're gone. I have all the warmth I need! P.S. we're on the fourth edition now. Jaylin Jr.

I know you all remember me saying I was going back for my son. Even though Junior made it clear he doesn't need me anymore, He's shit out of luck. I'm his fucking mother and I resent how quick Jaylin moved on after our divorce.

That shit was so embarrassing; I had to delete all of my social media acounts. The deadbeat mom comments and threats to slap the stupid out of me became reduculous.

I have a date lined up tonight with a sexy sugar daddy! At the same time, I have to be careful. I'll never give my heart to anyone else! Hell, apparently, I don't have one. However, this man is wearing me down.

I've been dating Nario and entertaining a few other gentlemen for a few months now. Though Nario is by far the sexiest man I've seen on this island, he's become a little clingy. Nario has one of those extra-long and thick sausages I had to pretend I could handle! I literally have to soak my pussy in the tub after our sessions.

"Come on, baby, let me just hold you until you fall asleep." Nario pleaded. Nario took me out on his boat in the beautiful waters of the Amalfi Coast. This is where I plan to live with my son! I have a nanny on standby, so I'll still be free to do what I want.

I almost gave in to Nario's offer until I realized the ladies I paid to snatch Junior haven't checked in with me today! Nario grabbed my waist and brought me to his hard rock body just before I opened the door! For a 51-year-old, Nario will put a 25 year old to shame!

A week ago, my neighbor from across the hall got drunk one night and blabbed about how she used professional baby snatchers to steal her baby! In her drunken state, I extracted the number from her.

During my research, I found that they had an excellent track record. The duo has never been caught snatching kids for people in losing custody battles, or women who can't bear children. Which meant I had to pay a pretty penny for their services.

Lingering in my doorway, the hairs standing up on the back of my neck weren't chills from Nario's touch. It was something else I couldn't explain at that moment!

"Uh, Nariooooo." I teased between kisses. "I'll call you tomorrow," I promised.

"Okay, my Bella Caramel." I froze at my name but brushed it off because Italians say Bella all the time.

"I told you not to call me that, Nario!" I gave him one last kiss and rushed to my door!

For now, I'm staying in one of the most lavish hotels in Italy and sinse the nanny isn't due to come and stay with us yet. I'm standing in the middle of the living room, utterly confused. I never leave my windows open, two I haven't smelled anything with floral scents becaus it makes me nauseous.

Three, there's a sparkly glass vase of lavender-tinted daisies sitting on the windowpane in a deep red wine-colored liquid. Also, a tall cake box sat on the dining room table decorated with an elegant deep sea-green bow and shiny silver wrapping paper.

I contemplated opening the box because it was not my birthday. However, Nario is forever buying me gifts, so this could be from him. Thus the reason for him wanting a nightcap! I ran to open the box and almost lost my bowels!

There inside the box sat two heads with their eyes gouged out. I picked up the postcard with shakey hands.

Here are your ladies who like to snatch babies
out of their warm beds.

Oh, how they sang like canaries before we cut off their heads.

Souls of our souls

You'll pay for the ones you stole.

You can run, hide and even nip and tuck

But the last thing you'll hear is.....

I stopped reading that awful poem and gathered my things to run! But when I opened the door, I felt my heart wind leave my chest! Ashton and Christian looked like two undertakers from a horror film, leaned up against the wall.

Suddenly, I notice Nario standing next to them with a grin on his face! "Oh. My. God!" I felt queazy as my memory shuttered before me! That's Angel's uncle Fernando! Flashes of desperate women tripping over themselves from the site of him at Angel's wedding played in my mind. How could I be so stupid?

Before I could utter a word, a woman with white hair appeared out of nowhere. My skin instantly turned cold, witnessing death in her ice gray eyes as she spoke.

"Green ones are my favorite!"

I was paralyzed by her irises as the last part of the poem loomed in my mind:

You can run, hide and even nip and tuck

But the last thing you'll hear is

PLUCK! PLUCK!

LOVE, THEE ELITE

THE END

Author's Page

I am overjoyed by the support and words of encouragement I have received from friends and family! This journey was difficult as I fought long and hard over my words. Growing up, I was one of the quiet ones full of surprises.

My roars were suppressed with pressures of imagery! Deep within was a creative mind moved forward in time. Poetry moved my soul. Spiritually inherited gifts of visions penetrated my mind! Yet my voice was suspended in time

Not wanting to be responsible for the could've, would've should've. My middle namesake shined through the darkness! Charlene remembers her good stories, and she is going to tell all of them! Buckle up!

Charlene Blue

Businesses Mentioned

Amili Williams

http://calilovepie.com/

Boojee Babies Bingo

Operator: Tamika Anderson

On Facebook

T- Shirt Label Creator: Lawrence Wilson (Rebel)

You can find him on

Facebook

Cover Design by Angel Jones

UP NEXT

KNIGHTLY FOREST

IF THESE DRINKS COULD TALK

Made in the USA
Las Vegas, NV
22 September 2021